Four Letter Words

NATALIA WILLIAMS

Quote in Chapter 23 from "Safe Love" by Francesca Lia Block, copyright 1999.

ISBN (print): 979-8-9887512-5-0

ISBN (ebook): 979-8-9887512-4-3

Book cover by Lucy Murphy, Cover Ever After

Editing by Andrea Halland

For anyone that has ever been 'in the biz'.
And for the old-school Buca crew, the best coworkers I've ever had.

ALSO BY NATALIA WILLIAMS

Taking the Cake

The Tango Series
Two to Tango
Four Letter Words

Four Letter Words

NATALIA WILLIAMS

AUTHOR'S NOTE

Four Letter Words is, at its core, my love letter to restaurants.

It tackles restaurant life from terrible bosses to amazing coworkers. From busy shifts to late night hang-outs at the bar.

There is a lot of swearing, a lot of drinking, and some physical/sexual harassment. You'll come across some Spanish dialogue, with plenty of context clues provided.

And at the end of the day, this is just a fun story about two bartenders that can't keep their hands off each other. I hope you enjoy it.

Thank you for reading.

PROLOGUE

Agostina

ABUELA PICKS UP A pen and begins to write, her signature loopy script dancing across on the page with each word. She was just at the San Diego tango festival with my grandfather—and her dance partner—Facundo.

Pure sunshine, she writes. *Gorgeous beaches, pure blue water I swam in. Outstanding food. Facundo found a delicious taco stand run by a couple from Tijuana. And then, tucked into a small corner, we found a bakery run by a couple from Corrientes.*

I've always been enamored with her sense of adventure. She travels constantly, flying to new cities, exploring in new places.

I can't wait until I get the hell out of here, too. Until I can see what this world has to offer.

I just finished writing an essay for my English class about what I would do if I took a gap year. Two detailed pages about traveling the world and savoring every second of it.

"What do you think you want to do when you get older?" she asks.

I shrug. "I don't know. I just want to see the world."

"Tu abuelo y yo, we got to travel a lot, gracias a Dios." Her leather-bound journal is filled with pictures and postcards of places she's seen.

"I don't need a fancy career."

She chuckles. "Como tu tía Cecilia," she says, likening my personality to that of my aunt—the fun one of the family, as far as I'm concerned. "No, you don't need a fancy job, but I hope you get everything you want, Agostina."

She gently sets her palm on my cheek and gives me a smile.

"What's your favorite place?" I ask her, flipping through each page, taking in every bit of information. I want to know all of it and more.

"That," she says with a smile, "I'm saving for the very last page."

One

AGOSTINA

"What's the ETA on the steaks for table 28?" I crash into the busy kitchen, yelling out the question as I tuck my book into my apron pocket.

My French braid is starting to come undone, wisps of hair unraveling from its once secured hairdo. Sweat beads at my temples, a headache looming in the far corners of my brain. I should probably get ahead of it, but I don't have a minute to spare right now.

My manager Steve put me on a party of twenty in the private room, and Danielle called out sick, so I'm juggling her section, too.

Can I do it? Of course, I can. I've been doing this long enough. The steps are memorized by now; my body knows the way to move by heart.

But I could still use some ibuprofen.

"ETA on the filets, Jose?" Chef Gary calls out.

"Two minutes, Chef!" Jose, the cook, calls out from behind the line.

"Filets for table 28 coming up in two minutes," Chef Gary repeats to me.

I don't have two minutes, but I grumble as I make my way

to place an order for a birthday dessert. I poke at the POS (point of sale, and frankly, piece of shit) system angrily, waiting for it to register and ring up my table's dessert. Pistachio cheesecake, tonight's special.

"I need some birthday singers, please," I yell out into what feels like the void. The term *birthday singers* might as well signal the plague with how quickly everybody disperses. I don't blame them. After a certain point, nobody needs the birthday song sung to them by a bunch of hot-mess waiters on a Saturday night.

"Come *on*! I don't want to do this any more than you do!" I shout.

"Fine," Manny, my best friend and coworker obliges, appearing from out of nowhere. "Where to?"

"Table 24."

"Alright," Jordan says, joining in. "Let's go."

The pistachio cheesecake is ready, elegantly plated and garnished with raspberries. I grab it, and they both follow me.

We clap and joyously sing happy birthday to the table, smiling from ear to ear, performing for our guests with the hopes that we'll get a decent tip. Everything is performative these days.

Once the song and dance are done, I drop the act and hurry back to the kitchen, gathering up my plates for table 28. Two filets—one medium, one medium rare—potatoes, grilled asparagus, and an order of the glazed brussels sprouts for two. I position everything on a large serving tray, squat down to adjust it onto my shoulder, lift up steadily, and walk out of the hot kitchen into the bustling dining room.

"Corner!" I yell as I make my way around, heading to my

section with table 28.

"One filet medium," I say as I set the plates down. "One filet medium rare. Grilled asparagus, potato gratin. An order of brussels sprouts," I recite as I place the sides in the middle. "Can I get you anything else?"

"No, thank you. This looks great."

"I'll be back to check on you in a few. Enjoy." My voice is calm and cool; I am the face of friendly and warm.

Once they're satisfied, I head back to the kitchen and drop off the tray. I reach into my apron pocket and rummage around for a small pack of ibuprofen, downing two with a quick gulp of water from the soda fountain.

"How you doin', T?" my other friend and coworker, Alexis, says to me as she comes up to the fountain and starts filling trays of drinks. She's got two large parties booked tonight, too, and we're both moving quickly through the restaurant, catching each other in passing.

"I'm doin'," I say in a hurry as I watch the orders from the party of twenty start to make their way up, ready to be delivered.

"Let's go, I need hands! Party is up!" Chef yells out. "I don't see you, T. Let's move!"

"Okay, calm down, Shein Gordon Ramsay." I roll my eyes as I watch Chef place the plates on the tray one by one.

Manny comes up behind me to help, ready to get the next tray.

A squat, an adjustment, a steady lift, and we are out of the kitchen again with plates for the large party.

I drop everything off with ease, placing orders in front of each respective guest, checking for refills, asking for any other necessities.

I reach for a pitcher of ice water nearby and top off half-full glasses.

"Everything looks great," the party host says with a smile.

I mimic her grin and nod, whisking away the trays as I head back to the kitchen.

I gulp down one more sip of water from the fountain, reveling in this quick break before I have to move again. My shoes are squeezing my toes, an unpleasant reminder that I've been on my feet for several hours now.

"How are you doing?" I ask Manny as he comes over to refill his table's drinks.

"Got some assholes tonight." He sighs.

"Table 37? Yeah, I can tell."

He huffs in annoyance but takes it in stride. It's all part of the job, unfortunately. Manny started here after I did, and he quickly became one of my favorite people to hang out with.

"So, what's going on tonight?"

I shrug. "I was going to meet this guy at New River Brewing, but I canceled." He was a Tinder match, and I don't think he's too beat up about it, either. He was attractive enough to entertain, but not interesting enough for me to follow through. Not that I've got the best standards, but I do have *some*.

"Always breaking hearts." He laughs. "One of these days, somebody is going to break yours."

"I don't think he cared. Besides, I never let it get that far." I wink, and he laughs again.

"Next door, then?" he asks, referring to the nearby bar that everybody goes to after work to wind down and hang out.

"Guess so," I answer as I look at the time and head back to my tables.

I catch Kelli in passing, and she stops me briefly.

"Hey, Blake wants to know if you can cover his Tuesday shift," she says.

"Why are you asking me?" I ask.

"He thinks you hate him and you'll say no."

"Having you ask me doesn't exactly make me like him."

She throws her hands up in question. "So, what should I tell him?"

"That he can ask me himself," I answer, stating the obvious, as I walk back to my section.

When I walk back, I notice a new two-top has just been seated in my section. Regulars that requested me, I'm sure.

"Hey, how are you?" I greet them. "I'll be back in one second," I say as I move to check on my other guests.

Every day brings something new, but some days, it feels like I can do all of it with my eyes closed.

Not that that makes anything easier. No, this job is always hard work. My feet ache, my body hurts. I get insulted, hit on, harassed, snapped at. I work for great tips and terrible ones. I miss holidays, I work through weekends.

But I'm not afraid of a hard day's work. My mother worked hard her whole life, gave us everything on the back of hard work. I'm proud of a hard day's work.

And I wouldn't have it any other way. Not when my best friends are here with me, not when my regular guests come to visit, not when I get asked to work behind the bar where I can socialize, create, and serve others.

The night continues in a blur. My party of twenty eventually wraps up, and I start to clean as much as I can. The bussers move the remainder of the plates out of the way, and I slowly work through the rest of it. My regulars are nursing their bottle of wine and thinking of getting dessert. Once they leave, I'll be done for the night.

As I'm cleaning up the remainder of the tables, Steve catches me walking back to the kitchen.

"T, I'm going to have you bartend tomorrow night," he says.

Steve has been playing Tetris with the schedule, moving us around however he can. We're down a lead bartender and charging into the busy holiday season.

"Sounds good," I say, reveling in this small victory for the position I've been asking about.

"I know we've been talking about lead bartender, so let's figure it out this coming week. We can talk some more and maybe see about making it permanent."

Finally, I think. "Thanks, Steve."

The wins are sometimes few and far between in this business, but I'm here for them whenever they come my way.

"So, where are you off to now?" Alexis asks as we're sitting at a table organizing receipts for the night. Her dark brown hair is pulled back into a ponytail, and her precise middle part is impressively still intact.

"Jersey. Just for a few days."

"Oh yeah? What the hell's in Jersey?" She laughs.

"Heard they've got good bagels."

"Bagels," she repeats flatly. "Alright then."

I chuckle. "I'll bring you back some."

"I love how you travel everywhere," she says.

I've been obsessed with travel since I was a little girl. Fascinated by airplanes and world maps, always watching travel shows and picking up travel magazines in doctor's offices. Everything excited me, everything made me curious. And maybe the feeling was stronger because I couldn't go anywhere, stuck in immigration limbo for so many years.

We came to this country from Argentina when I was just three. Tiny, adaptable, and resilient, as they say. Years were spent fighting for proper immigration status, a hurdle that felt farther and farther away the older I got. I know it was hard on all of us—my parents, and my cousins. We grew up together, taking on the problems together, and now we're all incredibly close. But we all handled it differently. And as for me, once we got out of the immigration limbo, once I graduated high school and turned eighteen, I was gone.

I crave new experiences and spontaneous days. I don't want a redundant, stale life.

"Steve's got me bartending tomorrow night," I tell her, a change in topic as we shuffle receipts and add them up.

"Good. Is he finally going to give you the lead bartender spot, or what?"

"Who knows?" I answer, but I secretly hope yes.

When I started working here seven years ago, there was a lead bartender in place. Erick had been here since the place opened three years prior. He left over a year ago, but not before he taught me some things and introduced me to our liquor reps, helping me build relationships with them. Once he left, I gladly jumped in to help cover shifts. But shortly after, the lead bartender position went to another server, Dustin. He redid the menu, gave cocktails stupid names, made a mess of things, and six months later, he was out. Again, I've been thrown in to cover shifts whenever I can, but this time, I'm getting that position.

"It's yours. It's gotta be," she says.

Alexis has been here for about five years. I trained her as a server, and we instantly got along.

The world always has plenty to say about the restaurant business and how it doesn't equate to a real job, but maybe they should work it for a while. Maybe it should be mandatory so they can understand how this work is hard and demanding and exhausting. How everything would fall apart without the hospitality business. But also so they can understand how you'll never find friends, make connections, find a second family like the ones you work with in the restaurant business.

If I ever need a ride from the airport, a lunch date, or some-body to run errands and vent with, I call them without question.

I stack my receipts together. "I won't trust it till I hear it."

"You deserve that spot. Even Trevor agrees with me."

"Trevor doesn't want lead bartender anyway," I say.

"Whatever."

I let out a deep breath, gathering my things. "Next door?" I ask her once I've finished my tip outs.

"I'll be there," she responds.

***

"Bagels? In Jersey?" Manny asks as he sips a beer.

"The real question is, ask her how many pairs of underwear she packs for a weekend trip," Trevor chimes in. He picks up a chicken wing from the platter in the middle of the table.

"At least six," Alexis responds easily.

"Five," Chad, one of the line cooks, says.

"Is everybody okay?" Trevor asks, appalled.

"I think I'm packing like six for this trip," I answer. "Alexis, you win."

She throws her hand up in cheer.

"Six pairs of underwear? Do you plan on shitting yourself?" Manny asks.

"Honestly? Maybe. You never know." I shrug.

"Women are so confusing." Chad shakes his head.

"And men aren't?" I take a sip of my IPA.

"We aren't. We say what we mean, and we pack appropriate amounts of underwear," Trevor responds.

"You're so full of shit," I say to Trevor with a loud laugh, while Alexis echoes similar words at the same time. "Who's playing?" I slip off the stool and head to the pool table.

"I'll play," Manny answers with a chuckle as he walks over to grab the other cue.

"Well, I hope for the sake of the women you two date that you always say what you mean, then," I say with a smirk.

"Are we talking about our dating habits now?" Trevor asks.

I give him one more laugh, a playful one, as we rib each other on. "You know I like my men emotionally unavailable."

"One day, she's going to meet *the* emotionally available one," Trevor tells the table.

"Yeah, and I'll make sure to say what I mean," I joke as everybody laughs.

"I'd pay good money to see T head over heels for some guy," Alexis chimes in as she grabs a chicken wing.

"Save it and come on vacation with me instead."

"Maybe one day," she says.

With that, I break the rack, and a stripe rolls into a corner pocket.

Two
GAVIN

It's NOT UNTIL I hear the key in the door that I realize I've been mindlessly scrolling through Netflix, not really watching anything. My brother Logan's back home, and I've done nothing since I got laid off a week ago.

It was a quick meeting, one that I knew was going to be bad news based on how everybody was acting. I should be upset, and part of me is, when so much of my life was spent breaking my back for a company that just cut me off. So much time was spent trying to cater to them for it to end this way.

"How was dinner?" I ask as he comes into the living room.

"Good. You sure you didn't want to come?"

"Nah, I was all right here. Where did you go?"

"This place called The Ivy downtown. It was nice." Logan met up with his longtime dance partner Tara. She's moving away, breaking up their partnership that has spanned numerous competitions and several years. My brother is a professional tango dancer, but he's having a hard time with it, too.

"Yeah?" I ask, but I'm maybe half listening.

"Yeah. And you want to know who I saw there?" He takes his shoes off and tosses them by the door. "Steve."

"Really?"

"I think he might be a manager."

"No shit?" This piques my interest.

"When's the last time you saw him?"

I tilt my head up to think about it. "Maybe four years ago?"

"Maybe...you could talk to him?"

I'm sure Logan is tired of seeing me on this couch, doing nothing with my time. I'm tired of sitting here myself, but I haven't wanted to move. I haven't had the interest to even look for another job. To go do what? The same bullshit I was doing before? With the same demands and the same crazy work schedule? Why even bother?

I worked for The Lehman Firm for eight years working my way up to a client relations coordinator. A fancy title for somebody who spent a whole lot of time on the road, on planes, in hotels. Selling the company, selling myself. I certainly made a living out of it, but the past couple of years left me wondering if the quality of life I was living was worth it.

I was rarely home, hardly able to spend time with Logan, let alone build decent friendships. God, I sound like a mess.

But listening to Logan talk about the restaurant, it's like he's pushing for a different kind of job. A different thing altogether.

"Huh," I say, now deep in thought.

I worked in some restaurants years ago. It's how Steve and I met. We always joked that the restaurant business was a place you could go back to. Down on your luck? Need extra cash? In between things and looking for something to do? Restaurants.

"What's the place like?" I ask.

He grabs a Coke from the fridge and comes to sit down on the couch. "It's nice. Down by Third Street. Good food, cool bar." He shrugs as he takes a sip.

Maybe I could go talk to him. It's time for me to find something new, something else. I was barely around enough to justify my rent, so I moved in with Logan about five years ago, but I want to have a life here now.

"I got a notice the rent is going up with the lease renewal," Logan says.

"Of course." I run a hand down my face, sighing in defeat. I can't live off the severance pay forever. Our landlord sucks, but we still pay less than most apartments in the area. I need to get back to work.

"I'll go talk to Steve next week," I tell Logan. "Thanks."

"Sure." He nods. "What are you watching now?" He points to the TV.

I've been sulking on the couch, going down a rabbit hole of random documentaries. Penguins in the arctic, koala habitats, Woodstock 99. It's been kind of relaxing. If nothing else, it's calmed my messy thoughts about what I should be doing and what I never got to do.

The layoff wasn't necessarily malicious, but it still stung, especially since I always got great evaluations. Even more so since I was a top earner for them. But everybody is replaceable, and I should have known better.

"Oh, nothing. You want to watch something?"

"Alright." He takes the remote and scrolls until he finds something, and just like that, we sit and watch TV together for the first time in years.

***

THE IVY IS NICE. Nicer than I anticipated. Part of me wonders how Steve ended up managing a place like this, but he did always have a certain kind of charm. Something that pushed him through the right doors.

Or maybe nobody else was dumb enough to take it.

The young hostess greets me with a smile. "Hello."

"Hi. I'm looking for Steve. Not sure if he's here?"

"Oh yeah. Sure. I'll get him." She retreats to go find him, and I silently, awkwardly, wait. It's busy for a Monday afternoon. Looks like lots of business lunches, a downtown crowd.

Can I do this? Can I jump into a busy restaurant again?

I hear him before I see him, a loud voice carrying over the din of the restaurant.

Steve looks the same as he did last time I saw him, walking through the space with an air of superiority that anyone could probably see through. He's harmless, but perhaps oblivious.

"Gavin Beck? Holy shit. Look at you, big baller!" he says with a smile as he walks up to me.

"Hey, Steve. What's going on?" I shake his hand. It's a little gruff and slightly sweaty.

Steve was never the greatest at his job, I'll be honest, but he was fine enough. Passable. And clearly worked well enough to move up to the manager role.

"You know, just living the dream." He motions to the place around him. "Last I saw you, you were traveling all around. Sales and shit, right?"

"Yeah," I answer quickly. "Nice place. How the fuck did you manage this?" I joke, and we both laugh. I'm easing into it, hitting the spots I know will work.

"You coming in to eat? Let me get you a table. It's on the house." He turns to go tell the hostess, but I stop him.

"No, no. Actually, I hate to do this," I say quietly, looking around, trying not to draw attention. "But I need a favor."

"Oh." He looks mildly concerned. "Shit, yeah, anything. You know I owe you one."

"I just..." I hate to say it out loud, but it's the reality of the situation. I tuck my hands into my pockets and ball them into fists. "I got laid off."

"Oh." Steve's eyes widen briefly. "That sucks, bro."

"I need something." A job. Here. "You can always come back, right?" I throw it in to soften the blow, but I realize I don't need to when I see Steve looking around and already making moves.

"You got it. Anything. Seriously, Gavin. I've got you. Hey, Manny," he calls out to a server walking by. "When is T back?"

"Wednesday," Manny the server answers then slips a glance at me before walking away.

Steve turns to me, thinking it over. "Can you start Friday?"

"Yeah, of course," I answer automatically, jumping up to the task.

"I'm putting you in as lead bartender. Think you still got it?"

"Oh." I still. "You sure?"

"Absolutely sure. I've got an opening I've been working to fill," he says like it's no big deal.

"Seems like maybe I should ease into it?" I chuckle nervously.

"It's nothing crazy, just working the bar, and I'll teach you about the bar ordering," he says breezily. "Listen, like I said, I've got you."

"Okay, well, I've still got it." I chuckle.

He reaches over to the hostess stand and grabs a business card and a pen. "Write down your number and email for me. Could you come by sometime this week to do your onboarding process? Quick stuff."

"Sure, sure." I nod.

I write down my information and hand it back to him, this feeling a little surreal. Everything started happening so fast from the second I walked in. I'm almost second guessing if this is even a good idea, but I take a breath and keep moving. This means a paycheck, and some breathing room, and a new start.

"Thanks, Steve. This means a lot."

"Don't sweat it. I'm happy to have you." He slaps a hand on my shoulder. "It's gonna be great having you here."

And with that, I head out with a new job and—even though one might argue this is a step back—what feels like a firm step forward.

When I walk in on Friday, there's already somebody behind the bar. A woman with light blonde hair is setting up wine glasses, carefully arranging them one by one.

It's quiet. There are some people sitting at the bar, I assume happy hour guests, but this is the lull between lunch and dinner. The calm before the storm of a Friday night.

I take a step forward then another. She hasn't looked up, and I wonder if she even knows I'm here.

"Can I help you?" she asks, organizing fruit garnishes.

"Oh. Hi." I give my friendliest smile. "It's my first day."

She looks up immediately, blue eyes staring right at me,

and gives me a once over. I feel stupid in this vest and tie, but everybody else wears them, too.

"New servers have to check in with Steve in the back office," she says, turning back to her fruit.

Just then, another person appears behind the bar.

"Hey," he says with a wave. "Trevor."

"Nice to meet you." I stretch my hand out for a handshake, still a habit and a formality from my previous job. Trevor hesitates before taking it enthusiastically.

His nails are painted a light holographic blue, and he's got a string of tattoos down his arm.

"New servers have to check in in the back office," he says, repeating the statement.

The blonde woman works on a drink order, moving bottles swiftly in her hands, tilting and pouring. She stirs the drink expertly then garnishes and turns around to serve to a guest.

"Who's that?" I say quietly and lift my chin in her direction. Another bartender, I assume. One I'll be working with?

Trevor laughs before mumbling under his breath. "That is our resident hard ass—for lack of a better term—Agostina."

"Don't you mean bitch?" she retorts, a smirk on her lips and ice in her voice, turning back to face us.

"I wasn't gonna go there, T," Trevor says with a chuckle.

"Bet you weren't," she says.

She turns her stare to me, an examination. I feel like a petri dish under a microscope. I'd feel uneasy if I didn't feel so intrigued.

"I'm Gavin," I say, breaking the silence.

"Hi." It's curt.

"Agostina?" I ask, clarifying to make sure I got it right. "Cool name."

Her eyes narrow at this. Suspicious? Confused?

"People call her T," Trevor chimes in.

"Oh, okay." I nod. "T."

"Want us to get Steve for you?" she asks.

"Oh. Sure. But I think he told me to meet him here. I'm the new bartender."

"Sorry, you're what?" she asks. Her tone makes it sound like that is absolutely not what I am.

"The...new bartender?"

She shifts her icy blue eyes to Trevor, and he throws his hands up in confusion.

The same server that Steve talked to the day I came in walks up to the bar now, building a slow-growing crowd of new coworkers I'm about to get acquainted with.

"What's up, everybody?" he says, but we're all in what feels like a standoff.

"Hey. I'm Gavin. Nice to meet you," I stupidly throw into the silence.

"Hey." He introduces himself. "Manny."

"Gavin is the new bartender," T says pointedly.

Just as his eyes widen to look over at me, Steve finally walks by the bar.

"Gavin! Hey, man. Perfect timing. What's going on?"

"Yeah, we'd love to know what's going on as well," T adds in.

He clears his throat, and I feel like I've just been thrown into a landmine. "I'm glad you're all here so we can make proper introductions."

"We've already been acquainted," she says.

"Alright. Well," he starts as he sets his hand on my shoulder. "Gavin here is our new lead bartender."

Trevor and T both look shocked and confused, and all I can do is stand there with a stupid smile on my face and hope nobody riots.

I know I'm the new guy. I know I'm walking into an established crew and I'm about to fuck it all up, but maybe I should have thought about this more when Steve handed me the job effortlessly and told me my first night would be a Friday.

The restaurant itself may be loud, a cacophony of plates and conversation, but right now, in this group, it is uncomfortably quiet.

Until one very particular voice breaks it.

"What the *fuck*?"

Three
AGOSTINA

"Why didn't you tell us about a new hire, Steve?" I ask.

"Why didn't you tell us you had somebody in mind for the position?" Trevor throws in.

"Since when do we hire outside for lead bartender?" Manny asks, entirely confused.

We might as well be a mob forming at the bar with how quickly we're throwing out questions. We've been here long enough, working together for years, and we always have each other's backs.

Meanwhile, Mr. New Hire, with his perfectly brushed brown hair and his stupid vest, looks on horrified. He should be horrified. Who the hell is he?

Steve has no backbone on a normal day, so I don't know how long it will be until he folds, but he throws his hands up instead and says to me, "Let's go talk in my office."

I slam the door behind me louder than I mean to, but at this point, I am fucking pissed. "Want to tell me what's going on, then?"

"Yeah," he kind of sighs, and winces, and has the decency to look a little apologetic, this asshole. "I meant to tell you before. He's an old friend, down on some hard times, and he needed a job." Steve takes a seat in his office chair, looking like his hands are tied. He can't possibly do anything else. A shrug in human form.

He looks extra sweaty today, and extra orange. Some days I wonder if he makes a habit of falling asleep in the sun, or if he's just too liberal with the self-tanner.

"So, you gave him the position you offered me?" My hands move to my hips, and my body rocks back and forth. Like the anger is moving through me so quickly I can't be bothered to stand still. I curl my hands into fists around my uniform so he doesn't see them shake.

"I owed him a favor. It was a whole thing."

"A whole thing?" My brain is about to pop out of my skull. "You hired your *old friend* for a position we always hire in house for. Specifically, one that was supposed to go to me. Do you hear yourself?"

There's a soft knock on the door, and Steve reaches over to open it, revealing a sheepish-looking Gavin.

"Hey," Steve drawls. "The man of the hour. We were just talking about you."

"Jesus Christ," I grumble.

"Look, I know this is less than ideal, but he's bartended before," Steve says, pointing to Gavin.

"You promised the position to me," I say to Steve quietly, a low tone so that I don't sound desperate. So that I don't give him any more to hold over my head.

"I didn't promise anything."

"We talked about it, Steve," I argue. My façade is cracking.

"Yeah, interim," he says, clipped.

That shuts me up. That's code word for not seriously. Not really. Not at all.

"Got it." I will not cry in this fucking office. Especially not with how Gavin is watching me.

"Steve, I can do something else if you need me to," Gavin offers, and it almost, *almost*, softens me up.

"No, no, Gavin. It's cool. Besides, I don't really have any other spots open." He winces.

"You could if you cut some of the dead weight," I mumble as I roll my eyes.

"It's fine. We can figure this out," Steve says as he sits up and thinks. We might expect some smoke here soon.

"None of this is fine, Steve," I say.

Just then, Trevor joins us, jumping into the office with his own confused expression, squeezing in next to me so I'm pushed against Steve's desk.

"Trevor, seriously?" I hiss. "This office isn't big enough for this fucking party."

"Sorry, sorry," he says apologetically. "What did I miss?"

"Okay, T, what if we switch you with Michelle and you take over the lunch bartending shifts?"

"She goes to night school. You know that," I answer. She works lunch shifts and goes to nursing school at night.

"Michelle goes to night school. Adam works at Roxy's on the weekends. Caleb is our backup." I list off on my fingers, giving him a clear picture of the mess he's made by throwing in an extra person and promising him this job.

"Okay, so how about this?" he says with a sigh. "Work together and let me see who's better fit for the position."

My eyeballs are about to fall out of my face with how hard I'm looking at him, eyes wide and aghast. "Seriously?"

"Steve, come on," Trevor throws in.

"We can use the extra help for the busy season," he tries to reason. "Let's get over this hump, and then I'll make my decision."

My mouth is set in a hard line. "This is shitty, even for you."

He sighs like he's so fucking weary and tired of my shit.

But I'm the one tired of his. I'm tired of being passed up for a job I know I'm damn good at in favor of mediocre men that know the manager. I'm tired of being pushed to the side, of not being taken seriously, of being asked to train mediocre men because they can't fucking figure it out themselves.

Steve came over from another restaurant about three years ago, which feels like ages in the world of restaurant managers. He started as an assistant manager, a mediocre one, inconceivably full of himself, dumb enough to take the position. And then he became a manager two years later.

And he's still mediocre.

And I'm still here.

Gavin looks over in surprise at how I'm talking to Steve. I guess to any newcomer it probably would be, but at this point I've known him way too long and I've been subject to too much of his stupidity to even bother with niceties.

I should quit right here. I should leave. I could find something else.

But why? Why should I? It's *my* job. He doesn't get to yank it away. I don't even know who this asshole is.

"Listen, I don't make the rules," Steve says, throwing his

hands in the air as he always does.

"That is *literally* what you do, Steve," I say, my own hands working in tandem with my words.

Just then, Jordan pokes his head into the office. "Table 16 wants a manager."

"Just figure it out, you guys. For starters, T, show him how we do things here," Steve says with finality as he gets up and follows Jordan out.

Trevor just sighs as he walks out after them.

Gavin and I are left standing there facing each other, his brown eyes meeting mine, apologetic, hopeful, maybe looking to extend an olive branch.

"I'm really sorry. I—I didn't know. I can leave, if you'd like." But the way he says it is shaky at best. He doesn't want to leave, and I don't blame him for that.

My eyes are ice, and I try to make them even colder as I stare him down and say my own final words. "This job is mine."

And with that, I walk out.

"Can you believe this shit?" I hiss to Manny minutes later when I find him getting his tables ready.

"Sure, I can. And so can you."

"I hate it here."

"You hate him. You love us. Remember that."

"Enough to stay here?" I ask it, but I wonder how much I mean it. This job has been part of my life since my twenties. I'm comfortable here, I have a whole hoard of regular guests here, plus flexibility and seniority. Starting somewhere new, especially in the middle of busy season and heading into the holidays, is a recipe for disaster.

"We'll chat later," I say sullenly as I leave him and make my way to the bar area.

As I'm walking, Steve stops me on his way back from Jordan's table.

"Hey, T. Listen, you're my best server. We've got big parties on the books coming up, and I would really like you to handle them."

I don't respond, giving him a hard stare instead. I know what he's really saying: think of the tips, the money that I'm getting you. It's not what we talked about, but it doesn't matter. I've already been pushed to the side.

Trevor is showing Gavin around when I make it back to the bar.

I love this bar. Its deep wood top and full shelves, its twinkling lights above me. Its patrons. This place is my home, everything comfortable under my hands. Glasses feel familiar, bottles I know by heart.

And as lead bartender, I want to make changes. I want to build something new—new cocktails, a new vibe. I want to make something lasting.

This bar is its own song and dance to learn, its own wild animal to train and tame.

And just like I told Gavin back in the office, this place is *mine*.

Four
GAVIN

"Look, how about we try to figure this out?" Trevor says hopefully in between us.

"Are you a spy?" T turns and eyes me accusingly.

"What? No." Maybe I expected this to be easier. I walked in with minimal hope and walked out with a job. But getting in the middle of it is different. Of course, it reeks of favoritism and bullshit, everything negative about the restaurant business. Of course, she's frustrated and suspicious. Steve practically told her the job would be hers.

"There's two hundred and fifty on the books. Let's just get through tonight," she says with an air of annoyance, or superiority, maybe both. "You've bartended before?"

Her question might be a jab. *Who the fuck are you? Where did you come from? Did Steve just put you here because you're his buddy?*

"It's been a while," I answer honestly. "But I'm excited to be back." That one is mostly the truth. I don't know if this was the right call.

She looks me over like she expects me to shrink from her stare, but I don't. I don't think I mind being under her watch.

"Maybe just watch to start, then," she says.

"That I can do."

She moves to set up wine glasses, carefully arranging them one by one. Her hair is pulled back into some sort of intricate braid. It's kind of fascinating to look at. I can't quite tell where the strands end and where they begin.

The shelves behind and above us are made of deep, dark wood and glass, holding bottles of liquor, with small twinkling lights woven throughout. The bar stools are plush, and they follow the bar all the way around. This place is nice. I can see why it's a popular spot for not only the lunch crowd, but the dinner crowd as well.

"We have service bar and bar guests." She reaches for a cocktail menu and opens it, pointing to different items. "We have a list of specialty cocktails we offer, plus some select wines and local beers."

I look through the list closely, trying my best to study it.

"It might take a while to get them all memorized. We do have a recipe book tucked over here if you need it." She reaches for a small, spiral-bound book stuffed in a corner, but it looks like it's rarely used. "A lot of these came from our previous lead bartender."

"Can we do our own thing?"

A heavy sigh rolls out of her mouth, and I can practically feel the irritation. "Sure, but maybe focus on learning the specialty stuff first. It's about 60% of our orders."

I nod eagerly. "Of course."

"The lead bartender can set up new specialty cocktails for the future. Sometimes Steve lets us showcase a drink of the day. Some of these cocktails are stupid."

"Dustin was only here for six months, but his presence is felt every day," Trevor says sarcastically.

"Dustin sucked," she adds in.

She walks along the bar, showing me how everything is laid out. "Fruit garnishes go here. We've got an array of glasses along this shelf." She points to a low shelf then shows me one above our heads. "And wine glasses hang here.

"Local beers in this cooler. Domestic stuff here. Imported here." She points to different coolers under the counter, showcasing how each is organized. It's clean and efficient. I'm almost certain she might have a hand in that. "Familiarize yourself with the local beers. They sell a lot.

"We have a couple of liquor reps we deal with. I know them, you're welcome to meet them," she says, but with a tone that might possibly mean *you can meet them, and I'll tell them you suck, too.*

"These bottles are mostly for decoration," she says, pointing to the decorative shelves above us. "We have a storage closet where we can access extra bottles of liquor, mixers, and shelf-stable stuff. Fruit is in the walk-in."

"What about dairy?" I ask. "Mudslides?"

"When's the last time you bartended?" she asks, almost appalled. "Pretty sure the last time I had a Mudslide was on my twenty-first birthday and most of it ended up in a puddle in the parking lot."

"Sounds like a good time," I joke.

She just stares, unamused, before muttering something under her breath and moving on to the next bit.

"Menus," she says, handing me some printed menus. "Happy hour, lunch, dinner, and Sunday brunch. We keep utensil set ups here, restocked often and preferably before shifts. Bussers can help.

"Daily checklist." She practically throws a clipboard at me. "Morning and afternoon checklists."

"Your lists?" I ask. They're relatively long and thorough.

"Erick's," she answers. "Original head bartender."

"Erick's presence is also felt every day," Trevor adds in.

"We liked him," T says this time.

"Be an Erick, not a Dustin. Got it," I say, maybe hoping to get a laugh out of them.

"Well, so far you're a Dustin, so…" she says with a shrug, and I snort out a laugh.

But then she stumbles backward, tripping over my foot, and her glare almost makes me shrink this time.

"I guess it's been a while since you've worked in a restaurant, so here's a little refresher. If you're going to sneak behind somebody without them noticing, don't. Say 'behind.' If you have a tray of food coming out of the kitchen and you're rounding a corner, don't take your chances. Say 'corner.' That way, you don't end up wearing the food. Got it?"

I vigorously nod. "Got it."

I look through the menus, the checklists, and the recipe book slowly, reading the information and trying to absorb as much of it as I can. Trevor and Agostina work around me, and I watch a pair that is used to working together, that know how to do it well.

"So, how's it going, T?" Trevor asks as he dumps ice into the ice bin. "Stomp on any balls lately?"

"Not unless you count your dad's last night," T retorts as she's organizing the barware.

Trevor laughs loudly. "Yeah, he probably would like that."

This gets a laugh out of her, one quick burst that sounds almost musical. I didn't even think she could laugh.

"Want me to show you the storage closet?" Trevor asks me.

"I'll show him," T interjects. "Your regulars just got here." She motions to a group of women that look like they've been here plenty of times.

"Sorry," he says to me. "Tried to save you."

"Shut up, Trevor," T says, which gets another chuckle out of him. "Come with me."

And so I follow. I'm as ready as I'll ever be to jump back into this, and luckily, it seems I've got Trevor on my side.

The storage closet is tucked away in a corner. It's a small space with large metal racks, just as T described, filled with extra liquor bottles, wine bottles, mixers, and garnishes.

"Lead bartender does the bar order," she says matter-of-factly.

"Steve mentioned he would show me how to do it," I say.

She huffs out a humorless laugh. "Steve doesn't know his asshole from his elbow, but he's going to show you how to do a bar order?"

"I...I guess?" I'm not sure how to respond to that one.

"Let's walk to the kitchen." She rolls her eyes and leads the way.

"Hector. Mikey," she says, introducing the dishwashers and reaching over to give one a kiss on the cheek. "Hector has been working here longer than me. He's got two kids, one of which he's helping put through college. And Mikey is still in college." She shoots them both a smile. "New guy." She points to me, explaining who I am, and they barely give me a wave. "Silverware goes on the bottom, glassware goes in the racks. Plates go here. Clean them off before placing them down."

"Got it."

"Thanks, guys!" she calls out loudly.

"Do you have any kids?"

She balks at me. "Uh, no thank you."

"Ah. Me neither."

"Line cooks." She keeps going, walking through the kitchen to the line. "Chad, Sebastian, everybody calls him Seabass, PJ, Lorenzo, Jesus, Dee, Sous Chef Tommy, and Chef Gary." It might seem impossible to remember, but I've always been good with names. Always been good at forming a relationship, a friendship, getting people to give in to what I was selling. "Everybody, this is Gavin."

"Hey," I say with a wave, giving my biggest, friendliest smile, but they just mumble it back, if that. T gets a rousing hello and goodbye, though.

"Good to see you, T," one calls out, and she gives him a wink in response.

"Back door," she says, pointing to a door in the back of the building. "Always assume the alarm is on. Do you smoke?"

"No," I say quickly, but I know what she's getting at. The restaurant business is notorious for employees who take one too many smoke breaks, sneaking out for a quick cigarette before running back in. Steve included.

"Do you vape?" she asks. "'Cause that's no better."

I shake my head no.

"Good," she responds, looking at me. And I wonder if that question was more for her own notes.

We make our walk back to the bar, and the sound of the printer goes off, indicating an order for service bar.

T pulls it off the printer, showing me the drink order. "Espresso martini. The current It Girl."

She gathers ingredients for it, and I quietly watch where everything goes. Another drink order comes in, and she moves into action.

She might want to bite my head off, but she's being much more gracious than I expected about this. But maybe she's playing nice because she has to, because she wants this position, too.

"How was your date last night, T?" Manny asks as he comes over to wait for his drink orders. "Did you meet up with that guy?"

I'm learning names quickly and finding out where everybody fits. Manny seems closest with T.

"I sure did," she says, shaking a cocktail shaker vigorously over her shoulder. "He took me to Roxy's down by the beach and he was rude to the wait staff. Absolutely the fuck not."

She pours the mix into frosted glasses and sets them out for service. Two espresso martinis, perfect foam, three espresso beans floating on top. I'll admit they look good.

"Thought it was one espresso bean?" I question.

"Three," she says. "Health, wealth, and happiness. Don't piss off the espresso martini drinkers."

She continues to work through orders, setting everything down on the service bar. Quick, efficient, focused. Servers come and go, but some linger, wanting to chat.

Once drinks have been picked up, she takes a breath. "Okay, I have to pee. I'll be back. Don't touch my stuff, Gavin," she warns before quickly walking away.

"Don't worry about her," I hear a voice say beside me. She's tall, brunette, with a flashy smile. "Samantha," she introduces herself.

"Gavin."

"Nice to meet you, Gavin. She's a miserable bitch," she says, in the direction of Agostina. "If you need anything, don't be afraid to ask me." She flashes one more smile.

I feel like I've been thrown upside down. It's been years since I've worked in a restaurant, and it might be a while until I get acclimated.

"You just don't want to be on her bad side," Trevor says with a smirk.

"Seems like it's all bad sides," Samantha mumbles.

I hear the printer go off, and I reach for it immediately to get away from that awkward interaction.

"Want to give that one a shot, Gavin?" Trevor asks.

An order comes up for a classic old fashioned and I think I can do this. Just then, Agostina comes back behind the bar and steps aside to watch.

I work as quickly as I can, still learning the set up and ins and outs of this bar. The glass feels vaguely familiar in my hand—cold and heavy, a handful of potential.

I twirl it once before shoveling in a hefty scoop of ice and setting it on the bar top. I reach for the bitters and sugar, count my pour of the amber liquid. A garnish of orange peel and some cherries. Like riding a bike.

When I set the drink down, for the first time in years, something feels *right*.

I smile as I present my drink.

"Not bad," Trevor says, nodding in approval.

"Fine," T says curtly, arms crossed.

A couple sits down at the end of the bar, and she begins to recite, "Penny and Neal. She likes a salad with her Bloody Mary."

"Like a literal salad?" I ask to clarify.

"No, like five stalks of celery, eight olives speared, two strips of bacon, two cornichon, and hot sauce. Also"—she grabs a pepper grinder from the bar set up—"extra pepper. Jenny likes a Bacardi and diet, two limes. Her friend Beth likes a vodka tonic with four limes.

"Carol and Bill." She points to a couple walking in. "A bottle of house red, cup of ice on the side."

I can do this. I just need a notepad and a weekend. I pull out my book and a pen from my apron pocket and start to jot it all down. She watches with interest, or maybe it's mildly disguised rage. I can't tell.

I handle a couple more drink orders, the easy generic ones, but for most of the night, I just watch. I watch them work in tandem. I watch her focus, her way with guests, her demeanor with those I assume are her regulars. Her straight forwardness, the way she looks like she could absolutely eat you alive. It's kind of amazing.

"And that's a wrap on Friday night," Trevor says as the night comes to a close.

"Great," I say with enthusiasm. An attempt at making

amends? I don't know, but they both look at me.

"We may have started off on the wrong foot," I begin.

"What gave you that impression?" T asks.

I try again. "I don't want us to have animosity between us."

"Talk to your bro Steve about that." She shrugs.

This is going to be much trickier than I hoped, but I won't deny the joy I feel in trying something new. In jumping back into hospitality.

I've got bills, and I can do a good job.

And maybe I'll be the villain, but I'm going to work for this position, too.

Five

AGOSTINA

I take my cash tips from the night and separate them as I normally do—savings and bills and travel jar. That last one being the most important.

When abuela passed away two years ago, we spent some time sitting in a room dividing up things. It was as awful as it sounds, going through belongings and deciding who was more worthy of them. She was a professional tango dancer, and depending on who you ask, she was one of the most important ones from the last century. Or one of the best to come out of Argentina. Or the best female tango dancer—which always bugged me, because she was great in her own right. But to me, she was more than famed dancer Celestina Rossi, she was my grandmother with stories that spanned decades. With a life that I have wanted to emulate since I found out what travel was, what the world was. What kind of wonders it held beyond the confines of my own home and my own city.

When we divided her things up, some pieces were hard to decide on, leaving space for some possible resentment to grow, but some things made it easier, like the list she left for the cousins.

We each got something to remember her by. At the time, my

older cousin Julie got something small, I barely remember what it was. But the more important gift was what came later—just a couple of weeks ago, in fact. My grandfather found a box tucked away in the closet that was somehow missed, labeled just for Julie. And just like that, she got my grandmother's tango shoes. The perfect recipient for that perfect gift.

As for me, I got her travel journal, filled with stories and photographs from her travels and her life. My one cherished, prized possession. I swiped her passport, too, while I was at it—worn and loved and *used*.

I reach for the journal on my shelf, flipping to the page for Jersey. The leather is worn but has held up throughout the years. Postcards and pictures poke out, and I delicately stuff them back in. I read her words, her elegant cursive weaving across the paper, and my fingers follow along, touching the pages she once did.

July. It was hot, much hotter than we anticipated, but it was a wonderful city. A perfect weekend getaway. A delightful tango community. The locals were welcoming, joyous and friendly. And they led me to Johnson's Hot Bagels for the best bagel I've ever had. Facundo and I must come back here one day.

In between its soft pages, I tuck in some photographs, some stickers, and my own notes: *Late September. Sixties in the evening. Delightful. The kind of place that warrants a weekend visit. Really good coffee. The best bagel at Johnson's Hot Bagels.*

When I flip the page, I land on the next city: Portland. I quickly read the page and make my own mental note to look it up later.

I close the journal up and tuck it back onto my shelf, signaling the end of one moment and the beginning of the next. I tighten my tie, adjust my fitted vest, and slip into my nonslip work shoes. Another day, another shift. A new day with Gavin.

A Saturday night shift can be a headache on its own, but with a new person to train, shadowing me, it sounds downright exhausting.

I'm still angry and still unsure of what to do. I need the money; it's my job. He shouldn't get to take it away from me, but I don't know if there's much use in trying to talk to Steve. All I can do is show him I'm the best person for it.

I take a deep breath in and head to my car.

***

"Hola, ma," I call out into the house. It smells like milanesas, crispy and pan-fried.

My mom looks up from mopping. Sundays are reserved for family and church, but Saturdays are for cleaning the house.

Her shirt has a hole right at her waist, right where she would lean against her work bench when she worked at the factory doing furnishings and curtains. A whole stack of shirts with that same exact hole, ones that she now wears to clean the house. That hole makes me sad. It reminds me of how hard she worked and how much fun and enjoyment she didn't have.

"Hola, Agos," she says, greeting me with a kiss on the cheek.

I follow her to the kitchen, where she washes her hands and finishes making my father lunch, like even after all these years, he can't be bothered. And why should he? This is all he knows.

Somebody else handing him a plate of food, somebody else serving him.

She married my father young, succumbing to a life of marriage and servitude. Some days, when I caught her feeling nostalgic, I'd listen to her tell me stories of how she wanted to be a nurse, how she wanted to help people. But once she married my father, it was out of the question. He preferred her at home, watching the children and keeping house. When we moved to the States, she did eventually go back to work—teaming up with my persuasive tía Maria—but that's because things were much harder here. There were still kids to raise, but bills had to get paid. My father grumbled enough about it, but I do think working gave her some independence that she needed outside of him.

Other days, when I caught her after one too many glasses of wine, she would admit that she had a lot of regrets in her life. I don't want those regrets. I don't want to look back and wish I had done more with my life, tethered to some relationship unable to do what I wanted.

No. I want to be free, to live my life exactly how I want to. Nobody gets to take my joy away from me.

I open the fridge and scan it for snacks, settling on some slices of cheese and a box of crackers.

"Vas a trabajar?" she asks, looking at me in my work uniform. "Always weekends, always nights." She shakes her head in disapproval.

I shrug as I chew on a cheese-topped cracker. Nothing fazes me about her comments; it's nothing that I haven't heard a million times before. It's nothing that I take personally.

If it were up to her, I would have been a nurse, too. Nurses also work nights and weekends, but that's not really what it's about. It's about the fact that my job isn't really a career. It's a male-dominated industry, it's tough, but it's nothing special. At least not to her. But she never comes to the restaurant and sees me work. She never shows any interest in what I'm doing outside of what I tell her. And now, I unfortunately remember, that I'm in a fight for lead bartender. Something she at least had some interest in hearing about. A fancier title, a better role.

My father is on the couch, lounging and watching TV. I watch my mother break a sweat as she plates milanesas with mashed potatoes. A plate for my father and a Tupperware for me. I wasn't planning on taking any, but I don't fight it. She hands it to me and as I prepare to leave, my father comes over to the dining table and dives into his lunch.

"Bueno, nos vemos mañana," I say, letting her know I'll see her tomorrow night for family dinner.

I barely give my father a wave, but he's too busy eating to care anyway.

***

"ALRIGHT, SO LET'S LEARN some new stuff today," Steve says as he claps his hands together in some sort of motivational move. "How are you doing, Gavin?"

"Doing great," he says with enthusiasm. "Ready to keep learning."

Gavin reaches over to move some of the fruit, as if he's

somehow already made himself comfortable here. There will be no comfort for this asshole today.

"Don't touch the fruit," I call out, watching him rearrange the bar.

"Oh." He looks down at the container of lime wedges in his hand. "Sorry."

"The limes go on the other side," I tell him harshly. "Trevor, show him where the boxes go."

Just then, Julie walks up to the bar and takes a seat. I lean over and kiss her cheek in greeting. My cousins usually come to visit on the weekends, unlike my parents, giving us a chance to see each other outside of our weekly family dinners.

"What's going on?" she asks, just as my other cousin, Delfina, joins her.

My cousins and I are very close—born in Argentina, practically raised here, close in age. There are five of us in total, including Julie's younger brother Dario and my older one Leo, but us girls have always stuck together.

I give them a brief rundown of the past two days: our new hire, his new job, his connections to Steve. I don't hide my frustrations or my disappointment. And they don't hide their clear infatuation with Gavin's sharp looks.

Shortly after, he comes over and introduces himself.

"Hi. I'm Gavin." He stretches his hand out for a handshake. Formal, professional. Some business bro that got laid off.

They gladly extend their hands in greeting as I roll my eyes. "My cousins," I explain.

He walks off to the storage closet, leaving my cousins and me in loaded silence.

"Don't," I say, already anticipating the comment.

"He is...good-looking," Delfi says.

Their infatuated looks just serve to annoy me further, and I mutter, "Christ. Pretty sure Samantha already dropped her panties somewhere, and Manny is suddenly upselling drinks." And then hiss under my breath, "And he's trying to steal my job."

Julie's eyebrows briefly shoot up, while Delfi lets out a delighted cackle. "I need some snacks for this show."

As I put their order in—the usual calamari and flatbread—I see Penny and Neal walk in, making a mental note to start setting up her Bloody Mary.

"Hey, did you guys meet the new blood for T to sink her teeth into?" Manny whispers between my cousins, nudging them with his elbow.

"Oh, we sure did," Julie murmurs behind her glass. They spend the night chatting and watching our tension-filled interactions. But Julie's eyes show concern, as they always do, for me.

"How's Babs?" I ask her, regarding her terrible boss at the law firm she works at. She's still making Julie's life miserable, yelling at her coworkers, uninviting colleagues from the holiday party. "She's so miserable." I scowl.

"I had a boss like that," Gavin chimes in. "It's never good to be in that environment."

All I can do is give him a hard look, wondering why he's injecting himself into a conversation between my cousin and me, but he just shrugs like he's so unbothered.

"Just giving my two cents," he says.

"You can keep them," I shoot back.

Trevor lets out a laugh as he pours a beer and says, "He's not afraid of you, T."

"I know," I mumble, watching Gavin from the corner of my eye as his mouth lifts into the smallest smirk, something that looks less salesman and more...real. "It's bad for business."

The night continues in a busy blur.

"Trevor, two New River IPAs, please," I call out, and he reaches down to grab them for me.

I line up glasses and make several cocktails at once, stirring and pouring and garnishing. I shake the cocktail shaker vigorously, I reach for bottles of wine, I twist and uncork like habit.

And all the while, I smile with customers. I laugh with them. I listen to stories, and we tell jokes.

Two friends are celebrating a job promotion—she's now the new vice president of marketing. A couple are on their second date. One guy just got stood up, and he's nursing a scotch.

I love this work, and some days I worry that I couldn't possibly do anything else. That this is all I know, my livelihood based on the ever-changing landscape of hospitality. But I remind myself people will always need to eat, and things will always warrant celebration. Girlfriends will want to chat over a glass of wine, and blind dates will agree to meet over dinner.

Gavin looks on as Trevor and I work, getting a lay of the land, itching to get in. I can see it; I can practically feel how he wants to be a part of this, too.

But this is my family, and I don't care for those who butt their way in.

Six

GAVIN

"WE'RE HEADED NEXT DOOR after this," T says to her cousins as she's putting away bar glasses.

"Want to join us, Gavin?" Manny asks.

"Where is it?"

"The Knotty Bar down the street," he answers. "Stupid name, but good food."

The after-work hang out. Maybe this will help me, and I can figure out how to fit in here. Maybe I'll see if Logan wants to join me.

The Knotty Bar is a dive, the most comfortable kind. Bad nautical theme, distressed wood bar, faded paper coasters. A good list of beers on tap, though, so I can get behind it. And judging by how everybody seems to know everybody here, I can trust that this place is its own kind of solace after a rough night.

As I walk in, with Logan beside me since he agreed to meet up, I spot a small group of servers from The Ivy surrounding the bar. Some give me a small wave or nod in greeting, but most ignore me—the new guy that got handed a position he shouldn't have.

Then I spot T.

She's leaning over the bar, calling out her order to a bartender who's clearly familiar with her. A knowing smile, like he'll give her whatever she asks for.

She's switched from her work shoes to flimsy flip flops that I can't believe are still intact after walking on pavement. Her toes are painted the loudest pink I've ever seen, but somehow, it fits. She's out of her vest and tie, and her shirt is unbuttoned and open, revealing a tank top underneath. She looks over and catches eyes with me before quickly turning back around.

"Hey everybody, I invited my brother, if that's okay," I say. "This is Logan."

T gives another small glance back, but her cousin Julie's look seems to linger. She introduces herself, while others mumble a bunch of "heys."

Bartenders place several orders on the counter—draft beers, cold bottles, some mixed drinks—and most of the crowd disperses. Everybody seems to be moving to the outside patio. I spot pool tables and some high bar tops just outside underneath the awning.

"We've got a table out back," T says to Julie, holding a handful of drinks as she walks away.

"What do you want?" I ask Logan.

"Whatever you get is fine."

I order two draft beers, and we take them with us as we head in the direction of the outdoor patio.

Once we step outside, the humidity encompasses us immediately. There are large fans in the corners, adding a welcome breeze, but the relief is short-lived. I spot T getting ready to play pool with Manny, and the other table has just emptied.

I follow Logan's lead as he walks over to the table with T and her cousins, and I wonder if maybe here I can extend some sort of olive branch.

"Anybody want to play?" I ask.

"Sure," Delfina answers enthusiastically as she stands, and we make our way to the pool tables.

"So, how's it going?" she asks, picking up a stick.

"Going all right." I look over at T and Manny, who are playing loudly, laughing and ribbing each other on.

She laughs softly. "Tough one, huh?"

"Your cousin or the job?" I ask before I can think better of it, but she just laughs louder in response.

"All bark, no bite. You never heard it from me."

"She's good," I say quickly, aiming to correct my previous statement. "Competent."

"She is," she agrees. "But she's been there about seven years. That's a long time, you know?"

"Wow. I had no idea."

A poppy song starts to play on the jukebox, and Manny and T begin to dance. I should probably be focusing on this game.

"I didn't know I was about to get thrown into a mess with the lead bartender position, though."

"She's been filling in here and there, and I think Steve made her believe she would get it."

"Yeah, sounds like Steve." I sigh as I aim for a side pocket and miss.

"How do you know him?"

"We worked together a long time ago. I was working a second job at a restaurant for some extra cash, but then I moved on."

"To what?" she asks.

"I did sales. Client relations. Client mergers. Stuff like that."

"So, you're good with people." She gets a shot in, corner pocket.

"I think so," I admit. "It's been a while since I've been in this business, but I almost missed it. It's a wild animal, that's for sure."

"Like that train wreck you can't look away from."

"Exactly." I chuckle. "Nah. I'm excited for this, I think." I don't know why I'm telling her all of this, somebody I just met, a family member of a coworker no less, but she's kind and welcoming. And I could use some of that right now. "What do you do?"

"I'm a surgical vet tech. Also, a tough job." She laughs, but this one doesn't have the same joy. It fizzles and fades quickly.

She misses a shot, and I look over to find T lying across the pool table to make hers. On her tiptoes, one eye closed, her braid coming undone across her back. Nobody else is fazed by it, just T playing pool, I guess. And then, just like that, the ball rolls into the corner pocket and she wins.

I look back at Delfina, who's been patiently waiting for me to take my turn, smirking like she knows something I don't.

"What's with everybody calling her T?"

"Oh, that. So, growing up, she didn't love her name, so she wanted everybody to call her Tina. And then in high school, everybody just called her T and it stuck." She shrugs.

"She's got a cool name."

Delfina smiles. "She's a cool girl."

In the end, Delfina wins, and I thank her for a good game. We walk back over to the table, where I find Logan and Julie deep in conversation. They seem to have hit it off.

I see if anybody else wants to join me in a game, but Logan just says, "See if she wants to play," pointing to Samantha, who's been staring off and on all night. I can keep making friends, not a problem. I walk over to Samantha and offer my friendliest smile. T doesn't miss giving me one big scowl as I walk by, and I can't help but laugh.

I'm not a combative person, but I can't help but want to push her buttons. It's almost...fun.

"Want to play some pool?" I ask Samantha.

"I'd love to."

There's a large group of servers and cooks, most of whom I met the past couple of days, out tonight. I listen to their conversations as we play, just on the outskirts of it. There's a lot of laughter and joy. Loud voices and quiet exchanges. If nothing else, I almost forgot what it was like to work in hospitality like this. The way you all become family, the way everybody becomes so close.

Our game is short, with me winning, and when I check my watch, it's just past midnight. Julie and Delfina are saying their goodbyes.

"Fine. Manny and I will keep this party going in your honor," T says while she and Manny cheers their beers.

I wonder if she'll be okay to get home.

She's surrounded by people, though. Trevor tells a joke, and everybody laughs. Alexis, Jordan, Manny, and even some line cooks are all together, engrossed in conversation, decompressing, a loud group.

I walk back to Logan, and I think maybe we should call it a

night, too.

"Ready to head out?" I ask.

"Yeah, I think so. You doing okay?"

I nod. "I'll go pay the tab."

Once inside, I cash out with the bartender just as T comes in to grab another round of drinks for the table.

"Hey." I stop her. "You need a ride home?"

The question seems to surprise her, or maybe it's the fact that I've approached her outside of work, who knows.

"No," she says simply as she grabs four bottles of beer by the necks, expertly intertwined in her fingers, and turns to walk away.

"No problem. We'll be back to mortal enemies tomorrow, though," I call out to her in a pathetic attempt at a joke.

And as she walks away, she impressively shoots me a middle finger, her mouth almost turned up into a smile. Something playful, something looser after a couple of drinks. Logan catches this in passing as he's coming over to me, ready to go home.

"Everything okay?" he asks, eyes wide.

"Yeah. Everything's good." I watch T join her group back outside, falling into the middle, blending right back into the crowd. "Seems like you hit it off with her cousin, though." I jab at him playfully.

I think the relationship between Logan and me is falling into a rehabilitation phase. At least, that's what I hope. I spent so many years traveling for work, away from him, from our place. And many more of those years working until late hours, sleeping in when I could. I feel like I owe him so much more than I've given the past couple of years. And I wonder, in a dive bar with new coworkers, after a long night of a new job, here with my brother, if maybe getting laid off wasn't the worst thing that could have happened to me.

Logan doesn't say anything, just shakes his head with a smile. I'll drop it for now. I've got my own messes to worry about.

I walk over to Trevor to say my goodbyes, extending my hand again. A goodbye handshake. A *pleasure doing business with you* handshake. Another habit.

Trevor takes it briefly but then stops me. "Hey. You don't have to sell yourself here."

I still. "Oh. Sorry."

"Nah, don't apologize. I get it. But you don't need the act. You don't need to convince anybody."

I self-consciously look around at my new coworkers and, like I'm somehow drawn right to her, I almost instantly spot T.

"Especially not her," he says with a laugh. "She hates the bullshit anyway."

"I just think everybody's feeling very suspicious of me."

He shrugs. "It's fine. They'll get over it. We hire friends and family all the fucking time. Some work out, some don't. It's all part of it."

"Well, I'm not a spy."

He laughs again. "I know you're not a fucking spy. You're just trying to do a job like the rest of us." He sighs. "I'm not going to blame you for Steve's mistakes. No offense, but he doesn't exactly have a ton of fans."

"Yeah, I know." I let out a small chuckle, and the tightness in my chest relieves itself slowly. "Thing is, I don't want to give this job up just yet. I want to work for it, too," I admit.

He nods as he lifts his beer in a cheer. "Well, welcome to this shit show, I guess."

I wave goodbye to the rest of the group, but most of them are too deep in conversation to even realize Logan and I are leaving. We make our exit and head home.

Once we're back at our apartment, Logan says quietly, "Don't repeat this, but Julie is a new student."

"Oh," I say with surprise.

"She doesn't want her family to know, so please don't tell her cousin."

"That won't be a problem." I shake my head. "She hates my guts, we barely talk."

"Good."

"Good?" I ask, mildly insulted.

"See you in the morning," he says, not giving any other explanation or apology as he walks to his room.

Welcome to the shit show, indeed.

Seven

AGOSTINA

"Here." I hand a small paper bag to Reagan, the hostess. "I was by Mariana's today, so I grabbed you one."

Reagan looks inside, and her eyes widen. "A dulce de leche croissant?"

"*Factura*," I playfully correct.

"Factura," she repeats, sounding it out. "Thanks, T." She smiles from ear to ear, and when I turn around to walk away, I find Gavin staring.

"What?"

"That one mine?" he jokes, pointing to another paper bag in my hand.

I don't give him a response as I turn and head toward the kitchen.

"Hey, Dee." I set the bag on her station. Dee has been at The Ivy since it opened, and she worked in restaurants years before that. A woman in male-dominated kitchens working through the boom of Food Network alpha-chefs, holding her own every step of the way. She's in her fifties now, and her hands hold the callouses and burns of a life on the line.

"Thanks, T," she says with a smile.

I admire her tenacity, scooping up some of my own from

her, and she deserves a croissant, too.

"Family Meal is up!" Chef calls out.

Everybody comes over to the kitchen, and we serve ourselves whatever they put together for the staff meal today.

Sous Chef Tommy made some flatbreads, Dee threw together a chopped salad with tomatoes, cucumbers, chickpeas, and a hefty mountain of pecorino cheese, and Jesus made a soup with some extra vegetables on hand.

I find a quiet spot at a corner table, and Manny manages to squeeze in next to me.

"I'm starving," he says as he scoops up a forkful of the salad. "County fair next week?"

I nod. "Yeah, sounds good."

"Alexis, you in?" Manny calls out to Alexis, who is sitting a couple of tables over.

"I'm not a fan of carnival rides that come out of suitcases."

"She's got a point," I say.

"I'll buy you a funnel cake," Trevor offers, nudging her with his elbow.

"Fine," she agrees, hardly putting up a fight.

Shortly after, Gavin walks over, spotting the open seat next to us, and sets his food down.

"Can I sit here?" he asks, looking right at me, making himself comfortable for whatever reason.

"You may," Manny chimes in enthusiastically.

I give him a sharp look before returning to my plate of food.

"So, how are you liking it so far?" Manny asks. So much for a quiet corner.

"Great," he says with a smile. "It's been great." But he's

shoveling more food into his mouth, chewing enthusiastically as he nods in approval, and it is driving me crazy. "This is really delicious."

"You are the loudest chewer I have ever met in my life," I say.

He just keeps smiling as he lifts his glass to take a noisy, unrelenting gulp of water.

"My *God*, are you parched from a seven-day trek through the Sahara? What the hell?"

"It's so easy to mess with you, T." He chuckles as he looks at me. He's got a sharp jaw. Not that I'm necessarily looking, but you don't see a jaw that sharp every day. He's got kind eyes, too, not that that's important.

I look down at my plate and finish eating.

"Anybody giving you a hard time?" Manny asks Gavin, and I close my eyes and pray for some fucking patience.

"Nah." He shakes his head. "I always appreciate the opportunity to learn."

I roll my eyes. The worst.

He smiles, and it's somehow softer than I've seen. That smile that's less salesman, more real.

Soon enough, he gets up and heads out. "See you."

But I don't respond, and with that departure, Manny zeroes in.

"Please, you cannot be blind," he says, exasperated.

"Blind to what?"

"I'm sorry. I thought hot and emotionally unavailable was your type."

"I didn't realize we had a welcome committee here."

Manny's eyebrow lifts. "The tension is bubbling. I feel it."

"Sounds like that's your IBS flaring up."

"Maybe he's worth breaking that no-coworker rule for is all I'm saying."

"Are you joking right now?" I set my fork down and lower my voice. "My *job*! He's stealing it!"

"If somebody that hot was stealing my job, I'd probably let them."

"You're ridiculous."

He laughs. "Obviously."

"Why is everybody on this asshole's side all of a sudden? Who is this guy?"

It seems like everybody is warming up to Gavin. When I walked into the kitchen earlier, some line cooks even asked if he was working today. Smells like betrayal to me.

"Okay, but really," he sighs. "He's nice, and he's in a rough patch. You know, his brother Logan's a dance instructor."

"Good for him," I say, clipped.

"Maybe he knows your grandmother," he says with a laugh.

"Okay." I put my hand up, sighing in annoyance. "First of all, dancers don't all know each other. Second, don't drag her into this mess. She would come in here and raise fucking hell about this."

He mumbles something in agreement then leans in. "I'm your biggest supporter, you know that, but we all know Steve's an asshole. And this is absolutely a Steve-made mess."

"That doesn't make this okay, Manny."

"No, it doesn't, but we just have to do the best we can with it." He takes a bite of flatbread, shrugging apologetically.

"And if I want to leave?"

"I wouldn't blame you, but I would miss you." He sighs. "I don't want you to go, T."

I grumble as I chew.

"The Agostina I know wouldn't let that asshole win."

"You just said he's so hot, I should let him take my job."

He smirks. "I was talking about Steve."

I shake my head. "I don't know if I get a choice."

"Don't make any rash decisions just yet. We want you here, and we all believe in you," he says, and I just look down at my plate and nod. "Love you, rubia."

I don't have much of an appetite left, so I gather my things and get up to go.

"Farmer's market this weekend, right?" I call out to Alexis as she finishes her meal.

"Definitely."

I make my way to the bar and get ready for my own busy night, but like clockwork, Steve finds me and approaches.

"Hey, T. I need help with the bar order. I know you've been helping with it, if you could take a look and see what we need."

I step back and look him up and down. The fucking nerve. "We agree how ridiculous it is for you to ask me this, right?"

"Yes," he sighs. "Could you just..." He passes me the clipboard, and I mumble some insults under my breath all the way to the bar.

We get deliveries twice a week, and making a proper bar order depends on the parties we have on the books, the beer and wine that have been selling, and any specialty cocktails we choose to feature.

It's not surgery by any means, but it should be methodical.

"What's that?" Gavin asks.

"Bar order," I answer, not looking up from the clipboard as I go down the list.

"Oh, can you show me?"

I'd rather eat nails than show you.

But he walks over, hopeful puppy face, with his notebook and pen in hand ready to take notes. He does appreciate every opportunity to learn, and I wish I could just call him a monster and get it over with.

"So, what do you like about the bar?" he asks as I continue to move down the list, offering points and explaining things as we go.

I eye him. "Well, it gives me the chance to create, to serve people. To talk to customers, build relationships." I shrug.

"I like taking care of people, too," he says.

"That's not what I said."

But he just walks away to greet a customer, stupid smirk on his face.

A familiar face comes up to the bar then, waving at me. "Hola, linda."

"Hola, Javier." I lean over and kiss him on the cheek.

Javier is an old family friend, one that they met in night school when they were learning English. He's been a part of my life since I was about five, a familiar presence during holidays and other family gatherings. He's big in the tango community, and so when he found out who my grandmother was, he got to meet her and become friends with her, too.

"You speak Spanish?" Gavin asks, surprised like everybody always is.

"She's from Argentina," Trevor chimes in, then, in his most obnoxious voice, starts singing "Don't Cry for Me Argentina."

"Shut up," I whine, shoving him in the shoulder, but he just laughs. I've had that song sung to me so many times in my life, I'd say at this point Madonna owes *me* restitution.

Trevor is a lovable pain in the ass. We've been working together for the last five years. He used to play bass in a local band, working weekdays at The Ivy. He parted ways with them, amicably he claims, but he still plays. He teaches guitar during the week and has been known to bring his bass to the bar. He also reminds me of my older brother, so it's nice to have him and that energy around when my brother isn't. The rest of my family—aunts and uncles and cousins—live in the same city, but Leo, my older brother, chose to move to a city about two hours away. Some space away from the family—not that I blame him.

"What other secrets are you hiding?" Gavin asks playfully.

"None you're worthy of knowing," I answer as I place Javier's glass of Malbec in front of him.

"New guy?" Javier says with a smile, motioning to Gavin. He sticks his hand out as he introduces himself. "I'm Javier, and I'm here a lot," he says with a hearty chuckle.

Gavin gladly takes it. "Gavin. Nice to meet you." Somebody else to shake hands with. He must be thrilled.

"So, you're bartending?" Javier asks.

"Yeah. It's my second week, so I'm still learning."

"You're in good hands," he says, winking at me, and I just shake my head.

Gavin smiles, turning to help two women who have just sat

at the bar. His smile lingers, widening as he greets them and passes out menus while highlighting some specials.

Secrets or not, that smile could probably get him everything he wanted.

The women lean in closer, a study in body language that screams *very interested*, as I set down two espresso martinis for service.

"Good evening, ladies," I greet them. "Gavin is new, so if there are any issues or anything else you need help with, don't hesitate to reach out to me."

"Thank you, but I think we're good," one of the women says, not looking at me when she says it.

"I think they're good," he repeats softly with a wink.

Fine. I'll just go fuck off over here, I guess.

"Do you have any local beers?" I overhear one woman ask.

"We have Sand Shark," he starts to list off.

"That's not a local beer," I chime in.

"Oh, right. Of course. I forgot." He smiles at them, and that's all that matters.

He's got the face, that's the thing. He's got charisma, he's got appeal. And he knows people.

That's all it takes.

I get told to smile more. To be friendlier. I get put in sports bars and get asked to pull my shirt down lower and pull my shorts up higher and maybe lean over a little bit, *honey*. He gets upscale restaurants, women during happy hours, men who trust his judgment on beer selections. I get business dinners with snapping fingers and handsy bosses.

And heaven forbid I ever mess up the local beers.

I stick to service bar for the next couple of hours, watching as he works. Keeping an eye on Gavin, that's all. But he's friendly and open. He sells.

And he keeps my fruit where I want it.

"This is a better place for it, you were right," he says as he's pouring a specialty cocktail, the unfortunately named Orange You Glad It's Friday. Dustin strikes again.

"I know."

"Makes my life easier."

"Well, that's unfortunate. I'd rather make it harder."

And maybe I don't realize in the moment how I say it, how the words spill from my lips, practically a waterfall of innuendo. Maybe I don't notice how I've been staring, but for a very brief, very unwelcome moment, there's the tiniest crackle between us.

And then I turn around and go back to work. Because fuck him.

By eight thirty, we've fallen into a busy rush. Raegan is sending more guests to the bar while they wait for tables, setting us behind.

"Sam, let's go, your drinks are piling up here," I call out.

"This is wrong," she says as she looks over the drinks, pointing to the old fashioned. "It's supposed to be Orange You Glad It's Friday." Hell, it sounds stupid even when she says it.

"That's not what you rang in." I hold up the printed ticket.

"Well, just fix it."

I stop what I'm doing and give her an icy stare. "You're going to wait now, Sam." The bar is filled, not an empty seat in sight, and these mistakes set everything back. "We've got a full bar here."

"Are you ever in a good mood?" she asks, annoyed.

"Are you ever good at your job?"

"You're a bitch."

"That's fine," I say, unbothered. "But I'm the bitch that's not going to hurry to make your drink just because you messed up."

"Ladies, please," Trevor interjects. "At least wait until we're all next door and I've got a beer in my hand so I can enjoy the theatrics."

"This is more drama than my abuela's telenovelas and twice as boring," Manny throws in, coming by to grab his orders and walking back to his tables in a rush.

"I'll make her drink," Gavin offers as he grabs the bottle of liquor and a glass.

"You're nicer than me." I shrug.

"Yeah, we know," Trevor teases.

"Thank you, Gavin," Sam says sweetly. "Is it hard to know somebody new can do your job just as good as you can?" she asks me with bite. "Or maybe even better."

My laugh is humorless. "We're all replaceable, Sam. Especially you."

Gavin sets the drink on the counter. "Here you go."

"Thank you for doing your job, Gavin," she says as she walks away.

My hands fly up in confusion and aggravation. "Does she ever do hers?"

The work relationship between Sam and I has been tempestuous from the beginning. She's much younger and got hired as a hostess in the beginning. Steve liked her enough to move her up to a server within some months, even though she'd never served—let alone had a job in her life.

I trained her briefly, but it was a struggle to get her to absorb the knowledge. Manny trained her after I did and did the best he could. Steve likes her too much to get rid of her, but I can only tolerate so many mistakes before I get frustrated.

Outside of work, I can admit we all have our flaws, but in the middle of a shift, on a busy Friday night, just do your job.

Trevor laughs behind me, and Gavin just shrugs because he doesn't even know what to do.

"Otro más, Javier?" I check in on him, and he nods. His friend has come in to meet him, and they're sharing some small plates as they chat.

I pour him another glass of Malbec and walk around the bar, keeping an eye on the guests. Who needs new drinks, who wants to eat.

It's a bustling Friday night, voices carrying throughout the restaurant, the kind of busy I love. It keeps me moving and creative. It keeps me talking, meeting new people.

We move circles around the bar, finding a rhythm as best as we can with a third person thrown in. But when Gavin moves to make a drink, he bumps into Trevor, and the glass flies out of his hand, crashing onto the floor.

"Shit," I mumble under my breath, while Gavin stares at the shards on the ground. "Broom is in the storage closet," I say loudly, snapping him out of it as he moves to the back.

By the end of the night, we're drained. I count out tips, evenly dispersing them between the three of us. And maybe for the first time, I'm genuinely worried that he'll take my job.

Manny comes over to settle his own tips, pulling out a receipt for his last table of the night. The ones that camped out, ordered waters, and left a mess behind.

"Oh, this is nice. They left me 10% and a coupon for rock climbing," Manny says, holding it up for us to see.

"Better than 0% and a religious pamphlet," Alexis comments.

"She has a point," I say. "Where's the rock climbing?"

"You would want to know that," Alexis jabs.

"I mean, it sucks, but seize the opportunity, I guess?"

"I wouldn't give them the satisfaction of my presence," Manny says succinctly.

"Fair."

He sighs. "It's that one you wanted to go try out."

"Ah, dammit. Well, I stand in solidarity with you."

"No, it's fine you can go." He waves away.

"I don't know. Isn't that like bad luck?" Alexis asks. "A shitty tip and a cursed coupon?"

"Like we haven't all been subjected to shitty tips," I reason. "Let's go commiserate over wings, and I'll buy you a beer."

We all meet next door again, but mostly so I can get a plate of chicken wings and an icy Coke.

"Busy night," Trevor says, sitting next to me with his draft beer.

"Yeah." I let out a deep breath, stretching my body, working out the aches and pains. "Want one?" I point to my plate of wings.

He thinks about it then grabs one from the pile. "Gavin is doing good," he comments.

"Unfortunately."

He laughs softly. "He helped out today. He even jumped in to remake Sam's drink."

"Couldn't be me." I shake my head, taking a bite of wing. "Mistakes every fucking weekend with her."

He mumbles in agreement.

"You're right, though," I tell him quietly. "He was a good help. I just don't know where that's going to leave me."

"What do you mean?"

"What if Steve has already decided to give him the job? What if there's no room left for me? Is this when I finally decide to go find something else?"

Too many questions and not enough answers.

Just then, our usual crowd fills the table. Alexis, Manny, Jordan, Chad, and even Gavin take seats, and the crowd gets livelier.

"What are you two chatting about over here?" Alexis asks.

"I think I need to figure out something with my eyebrows," I say as I take another bite of wing.

"What's wrong with your eyebrows?" Trevor asks, confused.

"I overplucked them in 2005."

"I'm telling you, microblading," Alexis emphasizes. "My cousin is going through beauty school right now. She can get you a discount."

"Please do not go get discounted microblading," Manny says.

"Whatever. My other cousin did it on a Groupon," Alexis mentions.

"Is that the same cousin that did a Groupon plastic

surgery?" I ask, concerned.

Alexis nods. "She loves a deal."

Manny looks over, wide-eyed. "Does she love her life?"

I laugh as I take a bite.

"She's doing great, but as for me," she says with a shake of her head. "You ever find yourself ass up in a stranger's bed questioning your life choices?" Alexis asks as she picks a chicken wing from my plate.

Gavin almost spits out his drink.

"Have you met Alexis?" Manny says, pointing to her.

"You single, Gavin?" Alexis asks, unbothered, and I hate how my ears perk up.

"Yeah." He nods.

"Casually dating?"

"Not really." He chuckles softly.

"Not your thing? I get it," she says.

"What's the scene with these dating apps anyway?" he asks. "Anything promising?"

"Depends on what you're looking for," Alexis says.

I keep chewing on my chicken wings, doing my best to look occupied, pretending I'm not listening in on this conversation that means absolutely nothing to me.

But I wonder what he's looking for. What a guy like him would be interested in. A housewife and a clean home, probably. Fancy plates and 401ks. Somebody to give up their dreams so he can chase his.

"I don't really know what I'm looking for," he says with a shrug.

"Well, you know, as long as you're not sending unsolicited

dick pics, you're probably okay."

"The bar is high these days, huh?"

"Some days, it feels like it's on the goddamn floor," she says.

"That's the fucking truth," I chip in, shaking my head, giving myself away.

"You got any Tinder advice for me, T-pain?" he asks, throwing in the dumbest nickname I've ever heard in my fucking life. Everybody else erupts in laughter, and his smug smile looks suspiciously victorious. A win in getting under my skin, it seems.

I narrow my eyes at him. Who the fuck is this guy? "Well, don't be yourself, that's for damn sure," I say.

"Noted." He laughs. "Anybody want to play?" He points to an open pool table, and Trevor stands to join him.

"Two peas in a pod, those guys," Alexis mumbles next to me, mouth full of chicken wing.

"Yeah," I agree.

The conversations continue at the table, several of them happening at once, but I listen half-heartedly as I watch Trevor and Gavin play pool. As Gavin makes a shot, his broad shoulders and lean figure hunch over the table. His nimble fingers hold his cue, and he's eye level and focused as he aims again. The ball rolls into the corner pocket this time, and when he stands upright, he catches me staring and smiles.

I sip my Coke and avoid his stupid smile for the rest of the night.

Eight
GAVIN

THE LAST TIME I was part of something like this, a close-knit group of coworkers, was the last time I worked in a restaurant.

A lot of it feels like starting over, probably because I am. Because I got pushed out of somewhere I thought I belonged, only to realize I never really fit in there in the first place. And now, starting from zero with a new job and new responsibilities and new coworkers, I feel like I'm getting it.

I get to laugh and tell jokes, share stories and food. I get to poke fun and serve guests.

And I'm starting to like it so much, it doesn't even matter that T hates me. It doesn't matter that sometimes I'll catch her scowling, because most times, I'll catch her just staring. And it really doesn't matter that I work in close proximity with her, because I wake up wondering what else she'll pull today. What new thing she'll yell at me about, what new lesson she'll teach me.

For some inexplicable reason, I want her to like me. I want to be seen as worthy of her time.

These are not just her coworkers, but her friends. The Ivy is not just some restaurant, but her place. And yes, she's very good at what she does, but what I really see is how this group is built on love and respect. They respect the hell out of each other, and they respect the hell out of her. And how could you not?

"I heard a server pissed her off so much she took his full tray of polished silverware and threw it at him," Blake says quietly, breaking me out of my concentration.

I'm restocking for dinner service, and it takes me a moment to realize his off-the-cuff comment is about T.

"Did your high school also have a pool on the third floor?" T says, coming up to us seemingly out of nowhere and leaving Blake practically terrified.

"I did hear you made Steve cry once," I add in.

This makes her almost smile, a twist of her lips like she's keeping from laughing. "Probably more than once."

Just as she says it, Steve walks up to the bar. "Alright. I want you two to work on specialty cocktails for tonight," he says.

Agostina once mentioned that he allows craft cocktails on a specials menu, and this could be a night that bumps me up a little. At least in her eyes, if nothing else.

I get to work quickly, moving to make something bright and bubbly. Something for the happy hour crowd, light and refreshing. Easy enough to drink multiples of while hanging out and eating.

Meanwhile, T moves slowly through the shelves, eyeing each bottle, making what looks like mental notes. And then she begins. Every pour from her is methodical. She moves gracefully, elegantly, like performing a delicate dance. I don't think she even breaks a sweat. She knows this bar like the back of her hand, and I almost have to stop to admire it.

She garnishes her drink with a basil leaf, and it looks like it belongs on the menu. Mine sparkles with fizz, executed to the best of my ability, as it rests next to hers.

"Alright, everybody. Taste test," Steve calls out to the servers on shift tonight who have gathered around. "Gavin, tell us about your cocktail."

"I wanted something light, something drinkable. I went with vodka, citrus, and prosecco."

The staff grab straws and take quick sips of my drink. The response is good, even better than good, as they rave about it.

"Really refreshing," Manny says.

"Light," Alexis calls out.

"Not too sweet," Trevor agrees.

"Great job, Gavin," Steve says.

T grabs a straw and gets her own quick sip in, and I automatically, unintentionally, hold my breath. She swirls the liquor around in her mouth, letting the flavors bloom, then swallows. She's quiet for a moment, thinking it over, before she says, "Needs something."

"What?"

"I said it needs something."

I dip the straw in and take a quick sip.

"What would that need? The flavors are good. Everything works together."

She reaches over the shelves, wordlessly takes a bottle of elderflower liqueur, and adds in a splash. She mixes it, the liquid making swirls in the drink, then offers it to me again.

And this time when I take a sip, the drink sings. Everything tastes well rounded, whole, harmonized in my mouth. I don't say anything, but I doubt I need to. Judging by the smug grin she flashes me, I'm sure she sees it in my face.

"Alright, T, tell us what you made," Steve says.

"I've muddled basil with strawberries and lemon, whiskey, and a hint of bitters. Served over ice, garnished with basil and a lemon slice. Let's call it Late Summer Sunset."

When I take a sip of hers, I don't know what to expect, but it's certainly not the layers of flavors that develop in my mouth. It's got the delightful sharpness of the whiskey, the earthy sweetness of the basil and berries, and the bitters that rounds it all out.

Maybe this has become a childish competition, something silly I'm following because I have to. But I'm starting to wonder what the end game even is when I'm working with somebody who is so talented, so clearly good.

Everybody raves. There is no other response that would make sense.

"Alright, what does everybody think?" Steve asks the crowd.

"Both!" Jordan calls out, and they all agree.

"You guys want to do both?" Steve asks us.

There's a beat of silence, like the room is collectively holding its breath, and then I say, "No. Let's do T's."

"Okay then," Steve says with a shrug, and T narrows her eyes at me. "Let's put it on tonight's specials. Everybody, upsell, please," he addresses the group.

The servers write down their notes on the cocktail, something to go by when talking to guests, and then they disperse to get ready for the night, and we move back to the bar to finish setting up.

Trevor refills the ice bins as he always does, T restocks the glassware, and I take to slicing citrus wedges for garnishes. As I'm slicing, the knife slips and knicks my finger.

"Shit," I hiss.

I grab a napkin and wrap my finger in it, but T has already noticed.

"Oh, hell," she says as she walks over to me, hand in her apron pocket. She pulls out a Band-Aid and wordlessly hands it over to me.

I stare at it for a second, then mumble, "Thanks," as I take it and wrap the bandage around my finger. And even then, I can't help but smile to myself. Unassuming Agostina with her apron pocket full of Band-Aids, ibuprofen, and extra pens.

She'll tell you she made Steve cry twice, she'll yell at Sam about her drinks, but the truth lingers right below the surface if you look close enough.

I don't think she has a mean bone in her body.

"Go sanitize that fucking knife, Gavin. You just cut your finger. Jesus," she says loudly, and I try to hide a smile as I move to clean the knife.

Shortly after, Steve is back. "Change of plans. T, I need you on the floor tonight. Party of thirty."

"Seriously?" she huffs, throwing her hands up.

"Yeah. Kelli and Danielle called out."

"Dammit," she grumbles. "Who am I working it with?"

"Just you. We're short staffed," he says. "Gavin, you'll be on the bar with Trevor."

I nod. "Alright."

Before T can argue, which she's opened her mouth to do, he walks away.

"For real?" she says in aggravation, looking between us.

We mumble apologies, but she just gathers her book.

"Trevor, can you handle the Late Summer Sunset, then?"

"Yeah. Write it down for me." He hands her a piece of scrap paper and a pen.

"Fucking hell," she mutters with an exasperated sigh as she writes down the recipe. "Grab some more basil and berries from the walk-in. Muddle it properly, please. Easy on the bitters." Trevor listens and nods as she gives direction, then she turns to me and says, "Hope you don't fuck it up tonight, bar boy," probably sending some curse my way.

One stupid nickname for another, and if Trevor catches me smiling at that, he doesn't say.

I missed this. The movements and the creativity. I vigorously shake the shaker above my head then tap it with my hand to separate and pour. A shaken cocktail, a spring of mint, and a lime wedge for a garnish.

I grab another glass, twirling it in my hand before setting it down and counting my pour. I lift the bottle as the alcohol flows out then I quickly bring it upright. A cherry garnish and an orange peel. I set both drinks out for service, proud of using my body in this way. The aches feel worth it.

And as I set them down, I catch T's eyes bouncing from my arms to my face.

"You're drooling, T-pain."

She scowls with an eyeroll and says, "Get me my drinks, please."

"Gladly." I roll my sleeves up another inch and play with fire just a little bit more.

I set her orders down quickly, flashing a smile. I don't miss the way she eyes my stubble, and my hands move to scratch at it, like I can feel her stare.

I can't remember the last time I grew out a beard.

I spent years at the firm with a clean-shaven face, shaving every other day. Polished and presentable, professional.

But here, there's flexibility, there's a looser attitude. When I noticed the stubble growing in this morning, I instinctively reached for my razor, but took pause. I didn't need to shave. I could comb my hair, wash my face, button my shirt up, and be just fine. So, I did.

"Oh, growing a beard, huh?" Sam asks as she catches me scratching it.

"Guess so." I laugh.

"Mm." She hums in what sounds like admiration, but this kind of playing doesn't feel quite like the cat and mouse game I seem to have with T.

"Keep it in your pants, Sam," Alexis chimes in as she appears at the service bar. "I need a bottle of the house red, Gavin."

"How many glasses?"

"Four."

I set four glasses down with her bottle, and she places it on her tray, moving quickly to her tables.

I feel like I'm falling into the groove, slowly sliding into the group. At least they tolerate me on the bar, which is enough. I hear the machine working behind me, the printing sound I've slowly grown accustomed to. But the sound doesn't stop, it keeps going. And going.

"Seriously, T?" I hear Trevor call out and turn to find him

holding a printed order of what looks like several drinks.

"Jesus," I grumble.

"Did I mention I'm really good at upselling drinks?" T says then briskly walks away, off to cause chaos who knows where.

Nine

AGOSTINA

Maybe I feel a little bad about it, dropping a bomb like that, but if he wants to be lead bartender, he needs to handle big parties and big orders. He needs to deal with time management and delegation.

So, as far as I can see, I did him a favor.

I guess he's growing a beard now. Or not shaving, I don't know.

It's prickly. It makes him look a bit messier, rougher around the edges. His forearms...well, I caught a peek of a tattoo under his rolled-up sleeve leading to who knows where.

As he garnishes the drink, his thick fingers make do, and my mind goes to *highly* inappropriate places. A sudden curiosity takes hold in my brain, wanting to know how he's used them before, who he's been with, how he made them feel.

Christ, no, thank you.

I redirect my thoughts. Like, what kind of tattoo would he have anyway?

Probably something dumb like his last name or his area code. Or something in a foreign language that he's got the wrong translation of. Maybe he's got a *Star Wars* tattoo.

Or worse, *Star Trek*.

I'm still drifting off in thought when I notice the drinks for my tables are starting to come up. Not a drop spilled, not a garnish missed.

"I'm missing an—"

"Espresso martini," he says, placing the last one down with a big grin. Foam top, three espresso beans, the It Girl.

"You're sweating."

"Just working hard over here, you know?" he says with ease and a smile.

I place my drinks on my tray carefully and head back to my table.

He's doing fine. Good, even. Well, my party of thirty is great, too.

"Corner!" I call out as I move around the restaurant, silently praying that these drinks make it to my table intact.

I deliver drinks to my guests, respective order in front of respective customer, and mention that I'll be back with the remainder. Twenty-four cocktails ordered, which is great for my bill, but tricky when it's just me running the party.

I head back to the bar for the remainder of my drinks, carefully placing them on my tray. A handful remain on service bar that don't fit, prompting a third trip.

As I'm doing so, a regular sitting at the bar catches me. "Hey, T! Are you being replaced or what?" he jokes, motioning to Gavin.

My smile is tight as I chuckle at his jab. I never cared for him much, but he mostly likes Trevor anyway. A bar full of men, that's what he likes, so he can talk loudly about sports and women and complain about how everybody gets so easily offended.

"Looks like you need some help, honey," he says loudly. "Let me help you with that."

And with my hands full holding a heavy, beverage-filled tray, I can't move away quickly, and I can't really fight back. He puts both hands on my waist—because that's exactly how you help somebody holding a heavy fucking tray—and acts like he's trying to fucking spot me.

"I've got it, Joe," I say firmly. "Let go of me."

"Hey, Joe," Trevor calls out. "She's good."

"I'm just helping," he says, defensively his hands slowly inching lower.

"You don't need to touch her to help," Gavin says sharply, the angriest I've ever heard him.

And next thing I know, Gavin and Trevor are both at my side, moving to get in between Joe and me. His hands quickly drop, thank God, and I take a breath. Gavin wordlessly takes the tray from my hands and starts walking toward my party. In a daze, I grab the remaining drinks that didn't fit on the tray and follow.

He stands at the head of the table, and I pass out every cocktail to its rightful guest. The party is loud and joyous. They recite appetizer orders, and I quickly write everything down, working with muscle memory.

"You good?" Gavin whispers to me, and I silently nod.

He walks with me back to the bar, tray in hand, and watches as I move in the other direction. I walk through the kitchen, past the line cooks sweating and shouting on a Saturday night. I move past the dishwashers working hard to get everything clean.

And I pull the handle to the walk-in, rushing into the cold, my eyes stinging with frustrated tears, and I let out one loud, curse-filled scream.

***

THE NIGHTS HAVE BECOME cooler, a comfortable seventy degrees that feels good against my sweaty skin. It was a busy night. It was an uncomfortable night. I don't like it when I feel my control slipping. When I'm so busy, I get so flustered, and I struggle to find my footing again.

I've experienced it before—the handsy customers—and I usually brush it off, because this is just part of my job and I can handle myself when I need to. But tonight, tied up with heavy trays of drinks and a large party, I couldn't. At least, I couldn't do it alone. Trevor has always had my back, but Gavin...

"Hey, you okay?"

I look in the direction of the voice and find Gavin outside, walking toward me. He had a busy night, too. His tie is loose, his hair is falling into his eyes, and his shirt looks rumpled.

"I'm good," I say.

"Does—" He clears his throat. "Does that happen a lot?"

"Not a lot."

He just nods. I don't feel like talking, but he doesn't seem to get the hint. He leans against the wall of the building, close but giving me space.

"It's been years since I've been in this business, and maybe I thought it would have gotten better. Probably naïve of me," he says softly.

"I can handle myself," I tell him.

"I know," he says with a sigh. "Nobody deserves to touch you like that without consent."

"I don't need the speech, Gavin. I live it."

"Right. Shit, sorry." He moves to go back inside, but before he heads in, he turns and says, "Trevor and I kicked him out, by the way. That guy can fuck all the way off. And if he ever comes back, I'll break his hands myself."

"Thanks," I mumble, humbly surprised, and he gives me a small, solemn nod before he leaves.

Ten

GAVIN

I SEE HER BRAID before I see her—loops and twists in that light, bright blonde. And then I hear her voice. It's softer than her normal tone, something more delicate, and that's what has me leaning over, listening in.

"How was today?" she asks whoever's sitting with her.

"Oh, it was fine," the person answers. But as I stretch my neck to get a look, I notice it's her cousin, Delfina.

"Don't bullshit me."

Well, there's the usual tone.

"It was, T. I promise. Tell me about your day. How's work going with Gavin, then?"

I can't help but perk up at the sound of my name, but I brace myself for whatever's coming. I didn't mean to give myself a front row seat to my own insults, but as I move over to listen better, inevitably curious, my elbow grazes a set of utensils that fall to the floor in a clatter.

They turn in the direction of the noise and find me sheepishly trying to hide.

Delfina snorts, a quick huff of laughter, but T just gives me a look of disbelief.

"Jesus. They let anybody in here," she says with a scowl.

"Gavin! Good to see you," Delfina says, and it almost masks the guilt on her face at my overhearing their conversation.

I can mask the discomfort, too, giving them a big smile and a wave.

"Come sit with us," she offers enthusiastically, moving plates and cups around to make space.

"I will haunt you," T mumbles under her breath to Delfina, but loud enough for me to hear.

"You were going to haunt me anyway." She waves the threat away, unbothered, then turns to me again. "We haven't ordered yet. Come on."

I didn't expect to see anybody here. I went to the Knotty Bar for a moment, but the work crowd was small, and everything just seemed too loud. I wanted a quiet night, and a late-night plate of food, so I came to this diner instead.

A server comes up to the table just as I make the move over. "More coffee, love?" she asks T.

"Yes, please," she answers. "Thank you, Roberta."

Delfina has a large mug of what looks like hot cocoa and a floating mountain of whipped cream. My mug is half-full, and the waitress doesn't ask me, just fills it anyway.

"Oh, he's not staying," T adds in quickly, but our server is already walking away.

"How come she asked you if you wanted coffee before she poured it?" I ask.

"Cause she knows it messes up my ratio, so she likes to ask first."

I watch T take the sugar container and turn it upside down, letting the sugar flow freely into the mug. She opens six creamers one by one and pours them into her coffee, slowly stirring until her coffee resembles the color of a beige couch.

"What is *that?*" I ask, appalled.

"Decaf," she answers unbothered.

"Not anymore, it's not." I take a gulp of mine, black and uncluttered.

"Figures," she mutters.

Our server comes back, holding her notepad and pen. "Okay, what are we eating? The usual, love?" she asks T.

"That would be great, Roberta."

"Fifi?" she addresses Delfina.

"I'll take the Belgian waffle plate, please."

Roberta jots it down quickly, nodding as she does. "What about you, hotshot?"

It takes me a second to realize she's talking to me. "The turkey club, please. With fries."

"You got it. Be right back," she says with a wink and a smile.

"I take it you're regulars here," I say, lifting my mug to take another sip of coffee.

"What makes you say that?" T asks wryly.

"Knock it off," Delfina says to T. "Yes, we've been coming here since high school. And she's the only one allowed to call me Fifi, so don't even try it."

"Well. Maybe one of two." T throws in with a smirk.

"Que gana de joder tenes," she says to T with a tone that can only mean something along the lines of *you're being fucking annoying.* It makes me laugh.

"How long have you lived here?" I ask.

"In New River?" T asks.

"No, in Florida. You're from Argentina, right?"

"We moved here when we were three," Delfina answers, and it just showcases how little T lets people know. How much I don't know about her, how much she keeps close to her chest. And all it does, unfortunately, is make me want to know more.

"That's awesome. My brother went a handful of times for dance stuff. He says it's beautiful."

"Didn't you used to travel all over or something?" T asks, and I almost smile at the deflection, and how she's thrown the spotlight back on me.

But the statement makes me flinch, like she wants special stories, too.

"What was it that you used to do?" she asks, awaiting an answer. Reminding me that I wasn't a bartender before this, that I was handed the role as an outsider.

"I was a client relations coordinator."

She scrunches up her face. "Sounds like a bunch of words."

I can't help but laugh. "Yeah, I guess it was."

"And what does a client relations coordinator do?"

"A liaison between clients and the firm. Customer relations. I dealt with a lot of clients, building and maintaining relationships, becoming a persona for the company."

They both look at me like they have no idea what I said, and maybe I don't either.

"That still sounds like a bunch of words," T says.

"How did you fall into that?" Delfina asks.

"It's just customer service, really. I got into it at eighteen and built a career out of it, I guess. I was good at it and helped support my brother. And at the firm, I liked maintaining relationships with my clients. I enjoyed the travel at first." I shrug. "It was a paycheck."

My parents lived paycheck to paycheck. There was never an abundance of money, just tight budgets, and the divorce didn't help things either. So, I took it upon myself to pay for Logan's dance classes and make enough to support us to get out of there.

"His brother is a dance instructor," T says to Delfina by way of explanation.

"Oh, I love that."

"Must have been a hell of a paycheck," T says. "Where did you travel to?"

This is Agostina outside of work. This is how I see her at the Knotty Bar. Manny once told me work is work, but the true testament of relationships is who talks outside of it. Who laughs and converses. I fell into this one, but it feels like I'm watching his words verified in real time. Like here we can forget that we're at odds in the restaurant.

"All over," I answer. "One of the last places I went to was Austin."

T's eyes light up with interest. "Did you go to Barton Springs?"

"No. No, I had to work."

"Did you see the bats?"

I clear my throat. "Also, no."

She furrows her brows. "So, you traveled to all these places but didn't even get to enjoy them?"

That's exactly it, but I won't admit that to her. "We're not all world travelers like you," I joke.

"Hardly a world traveler."

"*Such* a world traveler," Delfina repeats, leaning in, lightly teasing.

"You just went to Jersey, right? I've always wanted to go there."

She shrugs. "Then do it."

"It's that simple, huh?"

"Yeah," she answers, like it's obvious.

But it hits a nerve, like all of it is so easy. Like time and money are negligible.

"Guess you've never had responsibilities," I say.

She sets her mug down loudly, the noise echoing through the quiet diner that isn't exactly bustling at this time of night. "I have plenty of responsibilities, but I don't let them be excuses for the things I want to do."

She stares me down, as she always does, and I can't help but get lost in it. It feels like we're in a standoff—a really weird one in the middle of this 24-hour diner—but she quickly breaks it when the food arrives, a double cheeseburger and a heaping mountain of fries placed in front of her.

They both move like they've done this a thousand times before. Delfina reaches for the dispenser and generously pours syrup on her waffle, the sticky liquid pooling in the squares. T reaches for the ketchup and drizzles it liberally all over the fries.

My turkey club is placed in front of me, then Roberta proceeds to refill my mug again. At this rate, I'm never going to sleep.

"Probably should have gone with the decaf," I mumble, mostly to myself.

"Probably. Do you want your pickle?" T asks.

"I absolutely want my pickle, and even if I didn't, what makes you think I would give it to you?"

She shrugs. "Worth a shot."

"Anyway, you were going to talk about how much you love working with me. Before I interrupted, that is."

"No, I wasn't," she says, shaking her head as she takes a bite of a fry.

"So, you've been at The Ivy for a while."

"Seven years." She nods.

I give a low whistle. "That's a long time."

"Sure is." She takes another gulp of her coffee.

"You're good at your job, you know," I say.

"I do know. Thanks."

I can't help but chuckle as I take a bite of my own fry.

"Heard it was a busy night," Delfina adds, but the tone is softer, less enthusiastic. Agostina probably told her about Joe and her busy night.

"Yeah, it was. The bar is definitely tough. I admire how she's able to do it," I say in reference to T. "And she did great with her party, too."

Agostina keeps chewing, eyes on her plate, but Delfina watches her closely. Probably some sort of cousin code I know nothing about.

"Your cocktail was excellent," I tell Agostina.

"Yours wasn't terrible," she counters.

Delfina's eyes widen. "Practically a compliment."

"Thanks, T-pain," I say, and Delfina almost chokes on a piece of waffle.

"You're not welcome, bar boy," she says then takes a bite of her cheeseburger.

Delfina looks between us. "She doesn't even fight this much with us."

"How is work going for you, Delfina?" I ask.

T's eyebrows raise in interest as she turns to look at her cousin. "You told him what you do?" The tone is lightly teasing, a little disbelieving.

"It was fine," she answers, notably ignoring T's comment. "A busy day, lots to do. So, I agreed to meet for a late-night waffle." She nudges T with her shoulder.

"You never say no to a late-night waffle," T says.

"You know me too well." Delfina turns to me again, a forkful of waffle in her hand. "So, you're liking it, then?"

I nod, smiling to myself almost like a realization. I knew I'd tolerate it, I knew it would be fine enough. But the reality is, I *am* liking it. I am finding joy in the hard work, the conversations with customers, my coworkers. "Yeah, I really am."

Agostina takes another large bite of the juicy burger, the cheese oozing and running down the side of her hand. She sticks her tongue out and liberally licks it up, and I stop chewing just to watch. Eyes locked on the movement of her tongue, the lusciousness of her mouth. I swallow audibly.

She is objectively gorgeous, I can't deny that. She's fierce, she's strong, and right now, she's looking back at me like she would gladly bite my head off. And I'd gladly thank her for it.

"She's talking to you." Her voice registers, clearing through the fog, and she's pointing to Roberta.

I look up and find Roberta waiting, coffee pot poised and ready to pour. "Would you like more, hotshot?"

"Oh. No, no thank you," I practically stutter.

Roberta walks away, and I look over at my mug of coffee. "I'm surprised she asked."

"Honestly, you look like you need sleep," T says with what sounds like a slight concern in her voice. Maybe I'm hearing things.

I scratch my jaw. "I have a hard time sleeping some nights," I admit.

"We get it," Delfina says.

My eyes find T's again as she takes another bite of her cheeseburger, diving into it like it's pure joy. She never holds back, not with things that matter to her. Not with things that bring her happiness. Clearly the cheeseburger is doing it for her.

Or maybe watching her eat it is doing it for *me.*

Yeah, I need fucking sleep.

"I have to use the bathroom," Delfina says as she gets up and walks away.

The silence between us as Agostina and I eat is surprisingly comfortable. At least for me, anyway. Just unwinding after a long night, finding solace in company and quiet. But I don't think I ever feel uncomfortable with her, no matter how she feels about me.

I take a couple more bites of my turkey club, and when I look up, I think I catch T's eyes bounce from my face to her plate.

Delfina comes back to the table, phone in hand.

"I've gotta go," she says. "Emergency."

Agostina sighs in response. "At least you got to eat."

"I'll see you tomorrow night," she says, leaning down to kiss T on the cheek, then turns to me. "Thanks for joining us,

Gavin."

"Thanks for inviting me over," I say, but I'm looking at Agostina when I say it, inexplicably unable to look anywhere else.

"Don't look at me. I'm not the one that invited you," she retorts.

Delfina laughs as she waves goodbye to Roberta and walks out.

And with that, it's just the two of us left at the table.

Eleven
AGOSTINA

"Looks like it's just us," Gavin says.

"You're welcome to go back to your table now."

"This is my table," he emphasizes.

I pin him with a stare, but he just smiles. "Looks like everybody in my life has fallen for your obnoxious charm," I say.

He waggles his eyebrows. "You think I'm charming?"

"But I know you're just trying to get in with them so you can take that job."

"I like Delfina," he says, almost offended.

"She's not available," I quickly blurt out. Who knows why, it's not like I think he's interested in her.

"Not like that." He rolls his eyes.

Exactly. "So, you don't deny you're trying to take my job."

"I think we're both aware of the situation we're in." He sets his elbows on the table. "And besides, how is being nice to Delfina going to help me get that job anyway?"

I might be scowling again. "You've got some fucking nerve sitting here with me," I say, but the words don't carry as much anger as they normally do.

"I thought we were having a nice conversation," he says, palms up. "Was that just an act for your cousin?"

"Yes."

He smiles as he takes another sip of ungodly black coffee and says, "I don't believe that."

I sit back and chew on a fry.

"How long have you been in the restaurant business?" he asks.

"Long enough."

He sighs. "What's it going to take for you to open up to me?"

"Hell freezing over," I say without thought. "Probably not even then."

He doesn't respond, just quietly sits across from me. Elbows on the table, coffee mug in his hand, stubble scruffy. He's the picture of casual, of an after-work wind down. Of lowered armor. I give in.

"Since I was nineteen," I say. I wanted something flexible, where I could make decent money without being tied to a desk, without the rigidity of a nine-to-five.

"Why so long?" he asks.

"God, you sound like my mother," I say, laughing, not the least bit offended by this question. "My worth isn't tied to my job, you know. Everybody is so focused, so intent on building a career. On giving their life to a corporation for a paycheck, but what happens when everything is said and done? You look back and wish you could have had more time. More than just weekends. More time to do the things you love. I don't live to work, I work to live."

"I didn't mean it like that." His eyes soften as he shakes his head.

"I'm tired of everybody acting like nothing in my life is

serious. I make no apologies for the life I lead, no matter how much people want me to."

"Good. Don't apologize."

It almost trips me up, but I keep going. "That's what you got swept up in, didn't you? Giving up whatever for a paycheck. You said it yourself. So, you've come back to the restaurant business, and it's welcomed you with open arms. Steve sure did."

"I gave up a lot for a paycheck, you're right. And it didn't do me any favors in the end, but it kept a roof over my head and my brother supported."

He softens whenever he talks about Logan, I notice.

I lift my mug to take a sip. "What was the favor?"

He furrows his brows. "What do you mean?"

"Steve owed you one. That's why you got in. What was it?"

"Oh that. It was nothing." He waves it away.

"I find that hard to believe, considering he moved everything around for you."

He sighs. "There was a manager position open at the restaurant we worked at, and they had approached me about it. I didn't want it, so I told them to ask him." He shrugs. "It wasn't a big deal."

All that tells me is that Steve used it as leverage to get him in, to reason it away and keep me from the position.

"You could go work anywhere else," I say. "Go do your whatever job somewhere else."

"I don't want to," he says simply. "I want something different. I want something...rewarding. I know you know how that feels. When the night is done and your body hurts, but it feels good, like you worked for it. I love talking to people. And…" He pauses, thinking it over. "I think this is the kind of belonging I've been looking for."

I stop chewing. "Well, that was an earnest answer."

"Not used to that?"

"Thought you were a salesman," I quip.

"I was." He smiles. "Well, maybe I still am, but bartending has more of a lean toward earnest, doesn't it?"

"Everybody's therapist," I agree.

"And what about you? Would you want to find something else?"

I don't miss the way my heart races when he asks me that. Something close to stress, I'm sure. "May I remind you it's my fucking position, not yours."

"Well, technically it's nobody's position until Steve assigns one of us," he says pointedly.

My hand stills as I'm reaching for another fry. "I hope you choke on your turkey club. That's a terrible diner choice, by the way."

"It's actually delicious. Thanks for asking."

I sip my coffee and angrily watch him over the mug.

"You want that lead bartending spot, but do you even like it there? You yell at Steve every chance you get."

My eyebrows lift. Now I'm offended. "First of all, Steve deserves to get yelled at. And second, who are you to tell me I don't like it there?"

"I—"

"Shut up. That place is not without frustrations, I know that. They all talk about how I'm a bitch, how I'm such a hard ass at the restaurant. I know that, too. 'T is such a miserable grump, why would she even want lead bartender?' But I'm damn good at that job, and I'm allowed to want it. So, spare me your judgment as if you know anything about me. Because you don't. And frankly, you don't fucking need to."

I've been in this business a long time, pigeon-holed into certain characteristics, but I'm allowed to grow. I'm allowed to evolve and change my mind. Right?

He sits back in his seat. "I'm sorry." He runs a hand down his face, looking sheepish. "I swear I didn't mean it like that. I was just trying to figure you out, I guess."

"You don't need to figure me out."

"Yeah, well, I'd like to," he counters, looking right at me.

"Why?" I ask, but he doesn't offer up any response.

He doesn't need to know me, but whether I like it or not, I'm getting to know him.

"You really are good at your job, T," he says earnestly. "I knew it from the first day I met you."

"And yet I still can't get ahead."

Roberta drops the check in the center of the table, like a truce in this fight, and I reach for my wallet.

"Here," he offers, pulling out some cash. "You don't need to pay for me."

"I wasn't going to," I say, taking his money. "I tipped *you* out today." I set the money on the table, say my goodbyes to Roberta, and with that, we gather our things and head out to the parking lot.

Our cars are parked within a few spaces of each other. I lean against my car door and linger for a moment, legs crossed at the ankles. This is strange. Time has passed so quickly, the two of us diving into heated conversation, getting lost in it.

"Guess I'm going to go try and sleep now," he says.

And I know how it feels. How hard it is to wind your body down after a long, busy night. It's part of why we always end up at the bar, or why Delfi and I continue to meet here. I texted her to meet me tonight; I didn't feel like going out to the bar, but I didn't want to be alone, either.

Every night can start to feel the same, its own recurring habit. Go to the bar and talk loudly and laugh and close it down. Then get in your car and drive home with music blasting so the silence doesn't swallow you up. Go home and turn on the TV, letting the white noise fill the spaces. But you can't sleep for a while, so you let your body come down slowly, put your feet up to ease the ache, and wait until you can't even keep your eyes open. And you sleep in. And do it all again the next day.

"You're just getting back into it," I start, "but working in restaurants, it's hard to wind down, shut your mind off."

"I've had a hard time for some years now, but I know this business doesn't make it easier."

"Yeah, well..." I trail off, lifting a shoulder. It doesn't get easier. In fact, some days I wonder, as I get older, if I'll be able to keep up with it. If I'll be able to keep going at this pace, or if I'll fold and fall apart.

I've got lead bartender in me, part of me argues. But the other part questions, *yeah, for how long?*

I didn't want the rigidity at nineteen, but at thirty-three, would I prefer some structure?

My impassioned speech was true, but it's why I don't want

the silence, why I drown it out when I can. Because it creeps in and reminds me, loudly, The Ivy will not be my home forever.

And if it won't be, then what will be?

"You good?" Gavin's voice drags me back to the conversation.

"Yeah." I huff out a laugh to wave away the concern in his voice. "That's my cue to go. Goodnight, Gavin."

"Wow, did we just get along?"

"See you tomorrow." I open the door to my car and get in.

"This was a nice night. Look at us."

"Go to hell," I throw in for good measure, but his smile only gets bigger.

"Always a pleasure," he says, and if I didn't know any better, it sounds like he might actually mean it.

With that, I turn the engine and drive off, music accompanying me home.

Twelve

AGOSTINA

"You know nothing good could come from a ride called the Mega Hurler," I say, uneasy and queasy as we walk around the fairgrounds.

"Nothing a funnel cake can't fix," Trevor counters.

My stomach is about to revolt.

We spot the food stands, and Manny grabs a funnel cake for us to share while I grab the frozen lemonades.

"Alexis, you want one?" I ask.

"Yes, please."

"Anyway, so they left me thirty percent, which is wild," Manny says, continuing our conversation recapping Saturday night.

"That's awesome. My thirty-top was great. Easy-going, fun." I take a bite of funnel cake, the sugar coating my lips. "Joe stopped in."

"I thought I saw some commotion with him."

"He got handsy," I say, waving it away.

"He what?" Manny stops walking. "Are you okay?"

"He grabbed my waist. It was whatever," I say. "I mean, he's an asshole, but I'm fine."

"Don't downplay that, T. You should have told me."

"Gavin and I kicked him out," Trevor says, butting into the conversation.

"And Gavin said if he came in again, he'd break his hands," I throw in.

Manny practically chokes on his piece of funnel cake and reaches for a sip of frozen lemonade to wash it down.

"Speaking of Gavin, he's joining us." Trevor points, and we all look to find Gavin making his way over, balancing his own flimsy paper plate of food.

"Can I have no peace?" I grumble. "It's my day off."

"You'll live." Alexis pats me on the shoulder then takes a sip of her lemonade. "Hey, Gavin," she says with a wave.

"Hey," he says. "Hope you don't mind. Trevor invited me."

"The more the merrier."

"How's it going, Chuck Norris?" Manny says and I swear to God.

Gavin laughs quietly, tightly. "I feel like the better comparison might be Roadhouse."

These assholes.

He's dressed in a soft-looking long-sleeve shirt, those sleeves rolled up again to give a peek of tattoo. Sunglasses on, smile practically brighter than the sun, looking like—I don't even know, J. Crew after dark. He's got shorts on, and what is that—a 5-inch inseam? That is highly inappropriate for the county fair. There are kids around. I sneak a peek at his very toned legs and inwardly groan.

God*dammit,* I love a slutty thigh.

I'm scowling.

"Who's ready for the Twisty Whirl?" Manny asks.

"Absolutely not," I groan.

"Fine, I'll bite," Alexis answers, picking at a piece of funnel cake.

"Let's do it," Trevor says.

"I'll stay with you, T-bag. I don't mind," Gavin offers, and clearly I've just accepted my fate of terrible nicknames, because it doesn't even faze me.

"Thanks, but I don't need a babysitter."

"You two can do the Ferris wheel," Manny suggests, and I angrily take a bite of funnel cake and throw him my middle finger.

He mouths something like an apology, but I know he is not the least bit sorry as he walks away to get in line for the ride.

The line for the Twisty Whirl is long, so I make a plan to walk around the fairgrounds.

"Okay, well, bye," I say to Gavin and turn around to walk toward other sections of the fair.

"Hey!" he calls out behind me, walking to catch up. "Looks like it's just you and me."

"I didn't invite you to this one, either."

He laughs, and I don't want to think about how I've started to enjoy that sound. "Ah, come on. We're just two people, eating funnel cake, enjoying a day at the fair."

"Didn't take you for a funnel cake kind of guy."

"Didn't take you for a funnel cake kind of girl. Or a fun one, for that matter." He takes a bite of the cake, the powdered sugar leaving perfect little dotted imprints on his lips. His tongue peeks out to lick the sugar, one swift swirly motion. "You probably drink Steve's tears for breakfast."

I shouldn't find it so funny, but the laugh that bubbles out of me is both sudden and surprising.

He smiles in response. "I take it back. I'm sure you're a fun girl."

I glower. "Stop talking."

"You're right, that sounded bad. Anyway, I've been trying to go out and do things, despite my responsibilities. Like you said."

I assess him, chewing a piece of funnel cake, smiling at me. I can enjoy the fair by myself while the others hop on the puke rides, I don't have a problem with that. But, whatever.

"Fine," I grumble.

"Awesome. Ferris wheel, here we come."

"Oh, no, we're not going on the Ferris wheel."

"What? It's the best part of the fair," he argues. "And it's slow enough that it won't kill your stomach."

"You're obnoxious." I stuff the remaining funnel cake in my mouth as we walk, tossing the plate in a nearby trash can.

The heat is unrelenting as the late afternoon kicks in. I slathered my face with sunscreen, but I'm still feeling the burn on my shoulders exposed from my tank top. This weather should be illegal in October.

We walk through the dirt to the end of the fairground, where the Ferris wheel is set up.

We've all been coming to this fair for several years. Sometimes a group of us, sometimes just Manny and me. Always a fun time, even if my stomach can't handle the Twisty Whirl.

Gavin and I stand in line, waiting for our turn to hop on, and I have to wonder how I ended up with him by my side about to go on this ride.

We step up and into the seat, sitting side by side. The attendant locks the door, and we strap ourselves in, our hands brushing in this unfortunately tight space.

"I haven't been on a Ferris wheel in ages," he says, looking over the edge as we go up.

Manny likes them more than I do. He likes the view; I try not to look too far over the edge. But I wasn't going to tell Gavin any of that. He can assume I like the Ferris wheel, too. But as we go higher, the wind starts picking up, rocking our seat back and forth with stronger force.

I grip the bar in front of me, closing my eyes for a moment.

"Hey, are you all right?" Gavin asks.

I look over at him, and he looks concerned. Always aware, always a keen eye.

"Fine." Obviously, a lie. I don't know what's got me so nervous, but suddenly, we're one hundred feet in the air, rocking harder as the Ferris wheel comes to a forceful halt. Must be more people clamoring on.

Except, it doesn't eventually move like it would any other time. We stay put.

We're stuck. Jesus Christ, don't tell me we're stuck.

"I cannot be stuck here with you," I grind out.

"Yes, this is paradise for me, too," he deadpans. He leans over to look down, and it causes the seat to tilt.

"What the fuck are you doing?" I screech. "You're going to kill us!"

"Sorry! I was trying to see if I could get a look at what was going on."

"Pretty sure there's not much you can see from a hundred

feet, Columbo."

"Yeah, I got—Did you just call me Columbo? What are you, eighty-five?"

"Says the asshole making *Roadhouse* references?" I throw back.

"Patrick Swayze is an icon," he says matter-of-factly.

"Honestly, you're not deserving of Peter Falk's name."

He moves again, causing the seat to tilt back further, causing me to scream.

"I swear, if this Ferris wheel doesn't murder us both, I will," I say through gritted teeth. My knuckles are white with how hard I'm holding on.

"I'm sorry! I didn't realize they were so flimsy. They don't make 'em like they used to, I guess."

"Oh yeah? You spent your childhood days on Ferris wheels?"

"I was pretty popular in middle school," he says with that same smile.

"You're insufferable."

There's a loud commotion coming from down below. The attendant is yelling out something, but we're too high up to hear.

The frozen lemonade I slurped down earlier is doing me no favors right now. Can a girl really have no peace?

"Hey, so, I had some questions about the bar."

I turn to look at him in disbelief.

"Well, what else are we going to do while we wait? Sit in silence?" he asks.

"Yes."

The sun has started to set, casting the fairgrounds in a brilliant golden glow, and this high up it looks almost magical. This is the kind of romantic stuff Delfi loves. Unfortunately, my ride companion is less than ideal.

Except for those thighs.

No. Bad.

God, she'd probably lose her shit if she saw this. I pull out my phone, take a picture, and send it to her.

"Oh, is it selfie time?" Gavin says.

"No—" I start to argue, but he takes my phone like he's unhinged, turns the camera around, and takes a picture of us on the Ferris wheel. One hundred feet high, golden hour, his bright smile, and my shocked stare.

And then he hands it back to me like it was *nothing*.

"Your audacity knows no fucking bounds, does it?"

"Did you also watch *Matlock*?" he asks, ignoring my comment. "Were you a *Murder, She Wrote* fan?"

I huff in annoyance, rolling my eyes. I hear my mother's voice in my head telling me they're going to get permanently stuck like that one day.

"I'm not super close with my grandparents now, but when I was younger, I spent some time with them, and they liked *Matlock*," he says. "Personally, I think Angela Lansbury is where it's at."

It's one thing to be stuck in this death bucket, it's another to be stuck with somebody who's going to argue the merits of senior citizen mystery shows.

"I watched whatever was on basic cable as a kid," I tell him. "Along with telenovelas, but I can't imagine you know enough about those to make fun of me for them, so don't even try it."

If nothing else, I'm too annoyed to focus on the fact that we're stuck. And maybe that was his plan all along.

He's quiet for a moment, and we sit in silence as the wind swirls around us this high up, but then he breaks it.

"You all come to this fair a lot?" he asks.

"Every year."

He nods. "I don't really give a shit what anybody says about you, T." The words come out of left field, and I turn to look at him. "The right people know just who you are."

Our eyes meet and lock in a stare. What the hell does he mean?

"Yeah, I know," I say, automatically defensive, but my own words waver.

"I'm sorry that I've fallen into this role. And that I ask you questions because I want to know your opinion. And that I follow your lead because I want to do things how you do them. Everything circles back to you, because I respect the hell out of you."

I can't deny the buzzy feeling in my belly after he says that. *Motherfucker.*

Suddenly, there's a loud voice, a screech, and finally, movement.

The seat rocks again as it slowly makes its way down, and I close my eyes, inhaling one very deep breath. I feel a warm leg press against my own, not out of the ordinary in this confined death bucket, but I open my eyes abruptly and turn to look at him.

"I've got you," he says and keeps his knee pressed right

against mine as we make our way down. I keep my eyes ahead, watching the fair come into closer view, but I don't think he takes his eyes off me the whole time.

We stumble out of the seats and find our group standing nearby.

"Did you get stuck?" Alexis shouts.

"Sure did," I answer, stretching out my legs.

"The start of your own romcom, T," Manny adds in with a laugh.

"Yes, it was comedic gold."

"Well, who's ready for deep-fried Oreos, then?" Trevor asks.

"Oh hell, not me," Manny says.

"Trevor has a stomach of steel," Alexis tells Gavin. "I'll share some with you."

We make our way back to the food vendors, and I'm not oblivious to how Gavin seamlessly fits into our group. How they like him, whether he's my enemy or not. Whether he's here to take my job or not.

They find him funny and kind. They find him good.

Delfi replies to my picture with a whole bunch of heart eyes. How's the Ferris wheel with Manny? she asks.

Against my better judgment, I send off the picture Gavin took of us. Not quite Manny. Also, we got stuck.

She doesn't respond right away, probably because she's fainted on the other end, but then she sends back a very concise, rather shouty, BLESS THE UNIVERSE!

I send back a middle finger and then share a basket of fried Oreos with friends I love the most. I brush fingers with Gavin when we reach for the same one. He smiles at me and the inconvenient buzzy feeling in my belly only grows.

And as we walk around the fairgrounds, he says simply, "Thanks for riding the Ferris wheel with me."

Thirteen
AGOSTINA

"You asshole!"

There's a commotion on the line, followed by a rumble of laughter from the cooks. When I look over, I catch PJ plucking an anchovy from the handle of his low boy fridge. I'm sure I know the culprit, as I find Seabass in a corner, laughing his ass off.

The line cooks are full of pranks, most of which tend to involve fresh, extra juicy anchovies.

I practically run through the kitchen, grabbing plates for my tables and hauling ass into the dining room. I'm out on the floor again, handling some smaller tables and a couple of parties, including one in our party room. And this time, I'm in the fucking weeds.

I hate being in the weeds.

When I head back to the kitchen for another order, I hear Chef call out to me.

"Hey, T, 86 charcuterie," he says, holding up a printed ticket I just rang in.

"*Motherfucker*," I groan, speedwalking back to my table to deliver the news, and of course, it happens to be my difficult guests of the night.

"Unfortunately, we are out of the charcuterie board for the night." I throw on my most apologetic face.

"Well, that's just ridiculous."

"We do make everything in-house, but I apologize for this. Is there anything else I can start you with? The brussels sprouts are delicious. Or perhaps one of our flatbreads?"

She throws me an icy stare, and frankly, lady, I am unfazed by it. "Fine. We'll take a truffle flatbread."

I nod. "Again, I am so sorry."

Well, that'll affect my tip.

I walk back to the kitchen, pushing through the doors and into the heat and noise. "Hey Chef, can you get me a truffle flatbread on the fly, please?"

"Didn't know you were calling the shots tonight, T."

"Didn't realize you didn't properly prep for the night, Chef."

There's laughter from some of the line cooks, and a smirk from Chef Gary as he calls out, "I need a truffle flatbread on the fly, Dee."

Once I deliver the flatbread, they send me back for drink refills.

"Diet Coke and an iced tea," I recite, setting them down.

"Can we get new silverware? This one looks dirty." She points the fork at me, and I briefly wonder if she'll stab me with it.

"Of course." Another strike. "I'll be right back."

As I'm rushing to get new silverware, another table flags me down asking for drink refills. Once I deliver the silverware and grab the glass for the refill, another table asks for the check.

By the time I'm heading back with the check, I spot Carol and Bill from the corner of my eye, sitting in a section near the bar. I rush over once I've checked up on my problem table.

"I am *so* sorry," I say out of breath to them. "I'm swamped with the large party and some extra tables. I didn't realize you were coming in tonight."

"Oh, don't worry, honey," Carol says, reaching out to touch my hand. "We're being helped by him, and we are doing just fine."

They can't possibly mean who I think they fucking mean, and yet I know when I turn around I'm going to come face to face with him.

I turn in the direction of where she's pointing, and sure enough, it's Gavin. Standing straight, dressed to bartend, smiling that same stupid smile I've been privy to all week. I feel about one hundred feet high now, uneasy and hoping I don't free fall.

Nobody takes my regulars but me. That is the fucking rule. Nobody takes anybody's regulars.

I turn back to the table, restaurant smile plastered on my face and say, "Great. I'll come by to chat a little later, then."

"I have to head back to storage to grab a new bottle of the red, so I will be right back," Gavin adds, and then he's gone.

"He is just the loveliest gentleman," she says with emphasis, like a doting grandmother.

I am filled with even more rage as I turn swiftly on my heel and haul ass to the back.

"Who the *fuck* do you think you are?" I crash into the storage closet like the fucking hurricane they consider me to be, a swirling cloud of rage built up over everything that has happened up to this point. I slam the door behind me.

"Excuse me?" He looks appalled as if he has any right to.

"Why are you taking my regulars?"

"They asked for me."

"Bullshit," I say between clenched teeth.

"You were busy," he throws back at me. "They liked me, and so they asked for me."

"You don't just get to walk in here and take my tables and my regulars and claim it all as your own. You don't get to come in here"—my stupid voice almost breaks—"and take my *job* and claim it as your own."

"Hang on a second." He puts his hands up in defense, taking a step toward me. "T, it was never my intention to take anything away from you. I don't *want* to take anything away from you. I know this place is important to you, and I can't help that I knew Steve, that it brought me inside and allowed me to be part of this place. But you can't just keep it for yourself. What if this place is special to me, too? What if the people inside it mean a lot to me, too?"

"I'm glad you and Trevor are getting along so well," I say with bite, stepping closer, willing him to fight with me.

"Yeah, that's exactly what I'm fucking talking about," he says, aggravated and annoyed.

I feel it the second the tension shifts. There is something burning in here, unbearable degrees of heat that I thought were my rage, but now I'm wondering if it's something else. Something highly unwelcome right now.

But the way he's looking at me, sneaking a glance at my lips, is making me want. The way he steps closer like he's reaching out for me is making me want.

Our mouths are inches from each other, a devastatingly small space between us, and I am certain my body is leaning forward into his. He's mimicking it, that asshole, his chest grazing mine. Jesus Christ, what is happening?

If I don't put an end to this nonsense right now, something disastrous will happen here. My body doesn't get that memo, though, because it's still moving forward, happily meeting with his.

I'm so annoyed about all of this, so upset that I'm even here.

"I don't want to give you the privilege of my attention." The words slip past clenched teeth.

"God, it is such a fucking privilege, isn't it?" he whispers harshly, and I feel his breath skate across my lips.

I don't know who moves first or how or why or anything. All I know is we kiss, our lips meeting hard and passionate and fast. His hands brace my jaw, and mine move to grab his wrists. I don't even know why, I just grab the first thing I can reach to brace for this colossal fucking impact.

His lips are *warm* and *soft*, and what the *fuck* is this sorcery?

A groan slips from his mouth, lips parting, as his tongue makes its way into my mouth and I welcome it enthusiastically. This whole thing is such a reckless mess.

But I don't want to stop. Not even a little bit. He pushes himself closer to me, kissing me harder. An argument with our mouths, a rage building with how deliberate every move is. A fight with our bodies, a push and pull.

My back meets the shelf, rattling whatever contents are on it, but we don't stop. We don't even bother to come up for air.

Our bodies meet flush, and I feel every damn delicious inch of him against me. His hands move to my waist, gripping it with a strength I know he's capable of, and my stupid mouth betrays me yet again as it lets out a soft gasp. God, I want him tossing me around.

My hands move to hold on to his shoulders, my fists curling around them. He's so hard against me, and we're practically dry humping in this fucking closet. Christ, I'm going to rip his stupid vest with my bare hands.

God, this is so ridiculous. This is so absurd.

This is so fucking hot.

Suddenly, there's a loud crash, a string of curse words, and a mess of people outside the door breaking us out of this ridiculous trance.

We break free quickly, breathing hard. His lips are red and swollen. I don't even want to think about what I look like. Fucking hell.

I gasp for air, deep breaths I'm pulling from within me, and I watch him do the same.

What the hell just happened?

"T..." he starts.

I might imagine his hand reaching for mine, but I don't even entertain it. I open the door and storm out.

Shit shit shit shit shit.

I rush back to my problem table, checking in. Let them yell at me. Let them call for a manager. I need some sort of slap in the face over what just occurred.

But they're fine, tolerating the flatbread I'm going to remove from their bill. I refill drinks again, diet Coke and iced tea. I check on my party, moving to refill waters, checking for cocktail orders.

It's a miracle I'm moving as well as I am, because my body feels as stable as Jell-O. My heart is thrumming in my throat; my hands are too jittery. I don't trust myself to grab the cocktails, so I find Manny as he's coming back from his own tables.

"Help," I manage to say.

"You look like shit."

"I'm in the goddamn weeds. Help me with my drinks, please," I beg.

I must look like absolute hell, and when we make it to the bar to collect my cocktail orders, Gavin's eyes snag on my mouth. His tie is askew, and his vest is a little rumpled, and I know what his chest feels like under my hands now, and I am sweating.

I can still feel his lips on mine. Can still taste them.

When Gavin reaches over to start on another drink order, the rocks glass in his hand slips and shatters.

"One of those nights," Manny mutters, eyes wide.

"Must be a full moon," I say, almost absentmindedly. But fucking hell, this has got to be some kind of lunar nonsense.

Drinks get delivered; food is plated and served. I walk through the restaurant briskly, no corner left untouched, no section missed. Table 42 asked me for new utensils what feels like forever ago, and I run to drop them off, apologizing as I do. Table 46 just sat down, and I wish I could tell Raegan to chill out with the seating, but I don't even have the time to go do that.

Just as the tables sit down together, they leave together, and I scramble to print receipts and run payments. I can't wait for this shift from hell to end.

When I step outside, I feel like I can finally breathe, deeply inhaling the cool night air. The night isn't quite over, but I snuck out with the line cooks while they take a quick smoke break. It's past eleven, and I don't really feel like going to the Knotty Bar tonight. Manny is out; Alexis is out.

There's too much energy coursing through me, too much...stuff I need to rid myself of. The shift was relentless, and it didn't stop after that disaster in the closet, only amplifying with every passing hour until I finally caught up. Like some commonplace habit, I pull out my phone and open the first dating app I see, swiping as I go.

But nobody is catching my eye. These pictures are blurs of men I don't know and don't care about, warm bodies to occupy a spot in my bed for a moment. I close out the app, annoyed, and pull up Derek's number instead. I'm ready to text when a body slides next to mine. I look up to find the line cooks back inside and Gavin next to me, leaning against the wall.

"How was your night?" he asks.

"How do you think?" I shoot back. "That's two glasses you've broken, by the way."

He winces, scratching his jaw. "Yeah. I was a little distracted."

I look up at him, and his mouth unfurls into a smile.

"You want to talk about the closet?" he asks.

"You mean when you kissed me?"

"Pretty sure you kissed me first."

I can barely contain my irritation, unleashing a disbelieving laugh, but his smile grows in response, and my body, unfortunately, reacts. A swoop in my belly, an immediate answer to my frenzied energy, to my unremarkable search through predictable dating apps.

Maybe I can admit I'm physically—inconveniently—attracted to him. He is not terrible to look at by any means. I don't realize I'm slowly perusing his body until his voice breaks it.

"Going to the bar after this?" he asks.

"No."

He clears his throat. "I'm not interested in pretending that didn't happen, so…"

We've already crossed one line, and I can deal with the consequences of this later. For now, I don't care about any of it. I just selfishly want what I want. My toxic trait, my bad choice.

"I'm going home," I blurt out. "And you're welcome to join me."

His eyes immediately meet mine, searching for confirmation of what I'm asking. But he knows what I'm asking. We were both in that closet all over each other.

"Want to?" I ask quietly.

Gavin looks right at me and doesn't think about it much longer before he nods and answers, "Yeah, I want to."

Fourteen
GAVIN

"Huh. This is nice," I say as I walk into her small apartment. "I just figured you were like a wayward nomad living out of a box or something."

"Take your shoes off at the door," she orders. "No nasty restaurant shoes allowed here."

I walk around her place, eyeing every corner like I might find some secrets. There is so much color. She has art prints hanging up, loud and bright. She has a wall full of pictures thumbtacked or taped, and plenty more in frames around her apartment. Some plants in rainbow pots, half-burned candles on shelves.

This whole space is so indicative of her. She decorates however the hell she wants, and she doesn't give a shit if you like it or not.

When I had my own place, it was all clean lines and spaces. A place to entertain or impress. A façade. But this space is all her, and she's welcoming you into it like it's the highest honor. Like you should be thankful to even be here.

I walk over to the wall covered in pictures of friends and hangouts. Some from what look like years ago where she had bright pink hair and that same brilliant smile. Who even prints pictures anymore? Well, she does clearly.

"Want something to drink?" she offers.

"No, I'm okay."

She shrugs and gets herself a cup of water. I walk into her kitchen, feet padding on the tile floor. We stand in the small space, bodies opposite, watching the other. Her throat bobs with each swallow, and my eyes move to catch the rhythm of it. It's quiet, probably too quiet for her own comfort, so I break it.

"Why did you invite me back here?" I ask.

"Same reason you followed me here," she answers.

I chuckle, but I feel my face get hot. There's no denying an attraction now. Not after that situation in the closet, or every other interaction leading up to it. Frustration making way to infatuation.

God, I don't even know what the hell happened in that closet. One second, we were having a heated argument, and the next, I was completely at her mercy, kissing her desperately.

I walked out of it dazed and shaken, flipped over and fucked up. I don't think I stopped smiling for the rest of the night, even after I dropped the glass and it shattered all over the floor.

"What are we doing?" I want to hear her say it.

"Having sex," she answers simply, right to the point. "Just once."

I move closer to her, a repeat of the closet, and she watches my moves like a hawk.

"Just once, huh?" She's close enough to touch. "Why is that?"

"Are you looking for more?" she asks. "Did you set up that Tinder account?"

"I'm not on Tinder." I chuckle. "And no, I'm not looking

for a serious relationship out of this, T-pain.”

"Well then, we're on the same page. What a miracle."

"And just once is going to be enough for you, T-rex?"

"Oh God, tell your ego to shut up. Once is going to be just fine for me. You'll be the one unable to tame your hard-on for me."

This gets a laugh out of me. "Whatever you say."

She wraps her fingers around my tie and pulls. I offer no resistance as I move closer, as my hands rest on the counter on either side of her, caging her in. This close, my eyes study every inch of her face, linger at her soft lips, and finally land on her blue eyes.

I can't believe I'm here, in her home, amongst her things. She's been such a mysterious entity, only giving little pieces of herself reluctantly. And now here I am, in front of her, barefoot in her kitchen, wanting desperately to kiss her again.

"Just to be clear," she starts. "You can touch me. And I want this."

"Me too," I say.

I like the clear consent, the boundaries being set. I like all of it. And I like her.

She's still holding on to my tie, moving her hands up and down, like she's trying her best to straighten it. "And nobody needs to know."

I nod in a daze. I'm inches away from her mouth again, and it feels like we're teetering on the edge of exhilaration or ruin. I don't know which, but I want to find out.

"Want to kiss me again?" she whispers.

This side of her is intoxicating.

"Thought you'd never ask," I say with a smile, and then I lean in and press my lips to hers. It starts out sweet, delicate, soft, like it's our first kiss. Like I'm testing waters and I don't know how far I should go. But it quickly turns anything but sweet. Demanding, bordering on dangerous. I tilt her chin to kiss her deeper; I move in closer to feel all of her.

This might be out of my realm, one night with a coworker who I'll have to see regularly after this.

"We just need to be rid of all this stuff," she justifies in between kisses, and I don't have it in me to argue back. Whatever she says is enough for me.

"Whatever you say, T-bone," I joke.

"Shut *up,*" she growls as she grabs my vest with her fists and kisses me harder.

I meet her in the middle—messy, rough kisses like the closet.

My hands wrap around her waist, and I can't help but move them lower to cup her ass and squeeze. I'm not shy about any of it, and it seems like we're throwing everything out the window now.

She moves to unbutton my vest, yanking it off my body like she can't wait.

Her lips are soft, tongue meeting with mine. Before I realize it, we're moving across her apartment, barely stopping for a moment to catch our breaths. My hands still squeezing her ass, and hers fisting my shirt.

We stumble into the hallway as she moves us closer to her bedroom, crashing into a wall just outside of the kitchen.

"My conquests..." she starts in between a mess of kisses.

"Conquests?" I cut her off, appalled.

"...aren't usually this..."

"Good?"

We bump into a small end table and watch as her vase crashes to the floor.

"Catastrophic," she finishes.

"Shit."

"It was on a clearance shelf. It's fine." She pulls me back to her, but I take pause.

"Do you do this often?" I ask.

She pushes away to answer. "Does it matter?"

I study her quietly, and she stares back defiantly. Is this the end of the hookup? I imagine she's silently asking. What does it matter if I like casual sex? What does it matter if you're not the first to have been in my bed?

It doesn't matter at all. Not to me. Because she knows what she wants—she always does. And at this very moment she wants me.

"No," I answer clearly as I shake my head. "No, it doesn't."

And with that, I cradle her face and pull her to my mouth as we make our way to her room, bumping into the wall as we go.

She breaks away to turn on her bedside lamp, and the room lights up in a soft glow.

"This is awfully romantic of you, T-rex."

Her bed is a rumpled mess of pale pink sheets. There's something sexy as hell about it. I want to crawl into that mountain of sheets, burrow into them, and roll around in her scent like a dog.

She turns to face me, backlit by the lamp, and there's something sexy as hell about *her*. My eyes roam up and down, and

God, I'll never tire of looking at her.

"Come here." I reach for her shirt, but she pulls it off herself and tosses it to the side.

"Pants off," she demands.

"You're so bossy," I say with a smile.

"You like it."

"You bet your ass I do." I unbuckle my belt and pull it through the loops swiftly with force. "Take your pants off, too."

She unbuttons hers eagerly, kicking them off her feet. Long legs, lush thighs.

I swallow. "Look at you being so agreeable."

"You seem to be forgetting we hate each other," she reminds me.

"Right. Of course. All the more fun, then."

I take two steps toward her and lower my mouth to hers.

Fifteen

AGOSTINA

"Take this damn shirt off," I say as I fight with too many buttons, exposing the mysterious tattoo that starts at the crook of his elbow, snakes around his bicep, moves up to his shoulder, and ends at his collarbone. Vines and leaves and flowers. A whole delightful piece of art painted on his body, hiding underneath his buttoned-up shirt and vest.

"Fuck," I whisper, lost in the sight of it as I follow the lines up his arm, as my eyes get lost in the vivid color painted on his skin. "I...was not expecting that." It's not even *Star Trek*. I send up a silent prayer of thanks.

His lips quirk up at one side. "Did you daydream about my tattoos, T-pain?"

"Hardly."

Except as I look at his body standing before me—broad shoulders and strong legs, warm skin and a work of art along his arm—what I feel right now isn't akin to hate. My feelings are bordering on feral. I can't linger too long or else I'll never stop, and this is just a one-time thing. I can't give myself the satisfaction of more. It's just too messy.

I catch him staring at me, hair a mess, eyes wild. It's unnerving. "What?" I snap.

"Just admiring you." His voice is soft and delicate, draping me in it and drawing me right to the beast. "My imagination didn't do you justice."

"Did you imagine this?" I ask, surprised.

"Hardly." He smirks.

"You're so annoying," I say as I reach over to kiss him again.

We're back in a frenzy as I push him down to sit on the edge of my bed. I position my knees on either side, kissing him as I straddle his lap. There's barely anything between us now, just some thin fabric for underwear, and I can't even think straight.

His hands move behind me to unhook my bra, and his mouth replaces it effortlessly. My nipple is between his teeth, unearthing a rough moan from my lips, and I want more of it, but his mouth moves at a furious pace to kiss every inch of skin he can reach.

"I'm losing my mind," he pants.

"Good," I say, just as affected. My hands move to touch his face, roughly grabbing his jaw. "I want this goddamn stubble against my thighs."

"Fuck yes," he groans, kissing me harder. "I want you bent over this bed," he adds.

I waste no time in moving so that I'm on all fours on the bed.

"Fucking hell, look at you," he murmurs approvingly as he runs a hand along my thigh, following the curves of my ass. I push back against his hand.

He gives my ass a playful slap, but it's enough to feel right in my core. I let out a soft moan.

"Fuck," I breathe out. "Do it again."

He kneads my flesh then gives it another playful slap. He hooks his finger into my underwear and moves them to the side, and I curl my fingers into my sheets. My desperation is palpable, bordering on embarrassing, but I'm way too turned on to care.

"T," he says in a reverent whisper, and my answer is a sigh and then a whimper when his fingers slowly dip into me.

"Oh God," I groan.

His fingers are slow and gentle, exploring, and my body is too keyed up to function.

"You can be a little rougher with me, bar boy. I know you want to."

He wraps his other hand around my braid and pulls. "Is that right?" he rasps in my ear, moving to bite my lobe, the skin underneath, my neck. I can't help but moan in appreciation. "Fuck, I want to make you come twenty different ways."

"So, shut up and do it, then."

"You don't want me to shut up. You like it when I talk. You probably replay all the shit I say to you all day at work, don't you?"

"Pretty sure you're describing yourself."

He laughs. "Probably." He pulls my hair a little more, the sparks dancing through my scalp as his fingers dig in. His teeth gently graze my neck, and I feel his hard length against me.

"Fuck me, please," I practically pant. I sound like a mess.

"So polite," he murmurs. He adds in a third finger and pushes in deeper, harder. I moan louder against the sheets.

He pulls his fingers out and grabs my waist, rolling me over onto my back. "I want to look at you."

My underwear are twisted up and tangled, but he quickly

grabs them and pulls them off.

"Perfect," he breathes out, as he leans back on his heels to look at me. He really needs to stop looking at me like that.

"You want me to shut up?" he asks with a smile then bends down and puts his mouth right between my legs.

I grab his hair immediately and pull him down in reflex. "Oh fuck, you're good at that," I manage to say.

He lifts his head briefly, grinning as he says, "Just one time, huh? Guess I better make it count."

His stubble rubs against my thigh, a very intentional move, and it's so fucking delicious, I whimper. He's got me shaking on this bed. It's absolutely maddening how good he is at this. A passionate, unrelenting mess between my thighs.

I'm about to push him off me, for no reason other than I don't want to fall any deeper into this than it already feels, when my body starts to tighten. Wound up, building, an imminent explosion.

When I come, it's heart-pounding and surprising. Practically disorienting as I stare at the ceiling in a daze.

He sighs like he's so deeply satisfied with himself before grabbing my face and kissing me fiercely. I taste myself on his tongue, pushing for more as he moans into my mouth.

He stops for a moment, his forehead falling to rest on my chest, right between my breasts. "I don't—" He breathes roughly. "I don't have any protection."

"Top drawer."

He lunges for it, rummaging through a drawer full of condoms and toys.

"Oh fuck, we could have some fun here." He starts to pull

out some toys.

I sit up. "Not yours."

"Really? These are off limits?"

"Yeah. Now get a condom."

He grabs one, tears the package, and rolls it on. He grabs a hold of my thigh and gently moves to open my legs.

"Open up for me, then," he says softly, and it sounds hotter than anything anybody has ever said. His stupid deep voice and his stupid care and *dammit*. "Just once?" he asks, checking in.

"Just once." It's all I can handle.

He thrusts in, slow and deep, and all I manage to do is cry out, one pure sound of fucking ecstasy. It's not supposed to feel this good.

"You okay?" He looks concerned.

I nod.

"You're getting quiet on me now?" he asks incredulously.

"Yes, I'm fine," I manage through gritted teeth.

"Fine? I'm not going for fine."

"What are you going for, then?"

"I'd like mind-blowing. Explosive. Angelic." Each word is another thrust.

"Nothing like aiming really high, I guess." My breathing is getting heavier.

"Ethereal." His eyelids flutter as he moves in and out of me.

"Would you settle for better than most?"

He laughs loudly at that. "Be meaner to me. I fucking love it."

I don't want to think about how I still like the sound of his laugh, how it rumbles through my chest. How it lights up his face.

How good he feels inside me.

Our bodies are moving at a frantic pace, matching how wild we've both been since we walked through the door.

God, I feel like I'm choking on this fucking desire, this inconvenient lust. Drowning in it. I want him so much, I can't think straight right now.

I roll over on top of him, grabbing his wrists and pinning him to the bed. His eyes watch me, dark and hooded and like he's drowning in it, too. I hover just above then slowly lower myself onto him. My hips rock gently, a maddening pace that only serves to drive us both wild. Everything was so fast up until a minute ago, but I need this to slow down for a moment. I need to take a breath.

"What's up?" he asks, checking in on me.

"Nothing."

"Want to go slower?"

"A little bit," I admit.

"I like slower." He smiles.

And we move like that, slowly. I let go of his wrists, and he grabs my hips instead, rocking with me. He sits up and leans over to bite at the skin right under my breast. Then his mouth opens to suck.

"Are you giving me a hickey?" I gasp, my hands moving to hold the back of his head. "What the hell?"

"Nobody needs to know," he jokes, throwing my words back at me.

His tongue moves up to lick at my nipple, his mouth enveloping and lightly sucking. My body feels like it's on fire, heat pulsing through every inch of my veins.

I don't want slow anymore. I want fast again. I want out of control.

He matches my energy, moving with me as we both fall into a chaotic rhythm. I moan in satisfaction, and he hums in appreciation.

"Fuck, you're so perfect," he pants. "Keep going just like that."

Our bodies are covered in sweat, and his fingertips are gripping my hips.

He flips me onto my back, and when our bodies meet flush, there's what feels like an immediate spark. That sounds stupid. I don't know what it is, but it's an immediate crash on contact. And then his mouth meets mine, and the spark grows even bigger between us, the crash only serving to cause more destruction.

His kisses are wild and feverish. I ramp up my own speed, not wanting to stop kissing him, meeting his mouth with the same energy he's giving. His tongue is a divine feeling in my mouth. I wrap my arms around his back to pull him closer, and my thighs circle his waist. There's no space between us now. There's him, flush against my body, fucking me right into this mattress.

Suddenly, I notice the silence between us. No words, no bullshit back and forth. A reminder that I'm too busy fucking the enemy and enjoying it.

The words are easier, but this silence...this is falling into tricky territory. I can't let it go there.

"Still better than most," I tell him, right against his mouth, my own lips turned up in a smirk.

"You're not a great liar, but whatever you have to tell your-self, I guess."

This gets a laugh out of me. "Are you having a good time, then, bar boy?" I manage to get out, though I'm not sure how, because I'm very slowly getting there. Everything amplified, a tight wire running throughout my body ready to snap.

"I'm having a great fucking time, and I think you are, too." He thrusts in and then maneuvers his fingers between us to my clit. Jesus Christ, I'm going to explode. The moan that comes out of my mouth gives that away.

"You like that? Yeah, you do. I can't wait to see you come."

His words become jumbles in my brain. Now there's noth-ing but static and feeling and his fucking mouth meeting mine and then *there*. There it is.

I have to break away from his kiss so I can scream, loud and probably chaotic and...relieving. Like this has been pent up inside of me for way too fucking long.

"Holy fuck, baby. Look at you."

He follows with a thrust and a deep, rich groan above me, pulsing inside me which just makes me ride this wave longer. His mouth hovers above mine as we breathe harshly, as I grasp at his shoulders in lingering desperation. My hair has come undone from the braid and is covering most of my face, eyes peeking through strands.

Don't mind the fact that he called me baby. It was just the heat of the moment. Just words rushing out during an orgasm. We've all said dumb shit.

Doesn't feel dumb, though. Doesn't feel like just words.

This feels like I absolutely need to get him away from me,

and this most certainly will not happen again.

One time. That was it. It's completely out of my system now.

Look at that.

See? All we needed was a quick hookup.

He rolls over to lie beside me, and we both stare at the ceiling in what feels like the aftermath of a hurricane. My hair is a wild nest; he's panting. We're sideways on the bed and most of the sheets have come off the mattress, spilling onto the floor.

"I don't— I've never—" he says with each breath.

"Did I fuck the ability to speak full sentences out of you?" I say through my own deep breathing.

"I think so."

We're still coming down, breathing heavy, when he looks over at me and smiles. He smiles like he's the happiest he's ever been, and I don't know what to do with it.

So, I frown.

And then he adjusts the covers and lies next to me.

I still. "What are you doing?"

"Getting comfortable, move over."

"Uh, no you're not."

"Oh, I'm getting kicked out, huh?"

"Yes," I answer, like it's obvious.

He laughs. "Hot breakfast date?"

I feel bad kicking him out now. This shift is so subtle, and a little bit unnerving. I need him to leave. I need it for my own sanity, and I think he sees it too.

"Morning yoga with Manny," I answer. I don't owe him any explanation, but I give it anyway. A peace offering.

His grin borders on a smirk. "Alright, T, I get it. Just once, that was the deal."

He rummages the floor for his clothes, putting everything on quickly. I watch from my position on the bed, his wild state slowly being pieced back together, like coming undone in reverse.

Then he leans down to plant one soft, tender kiss on my forehead.

Christ, he needs to go.

"I guess...thank you?" he says.

Oh, dear God. "Don't make it weird, you weirdo!"

Gavin leans against the doorframe, hands in pockets, looking at me like he wants to say more. I'm not sure how much more I could handle. One more word from him, and I might tell him to just stay. I might break that wall right down and move over in this bed.

I don't need to get close to him, not right now.

"Night, T. This was fun." He taps on the doorframe twice, smile gracing his face, then turns to go.

Once I know he's gone, I lock the door behind him. And then when I crawl back into bed, I lie awake and stare at the ceiling fan.

And who the hell knows when I fall asleep.

***

I RUSH IN AND quickly position my mat next to Manny's. Luckily, class hasn't started, but I'm already sweating from the run I took from the parking lot to get here on time. Adriana locks the doors and does not let anyone disrupt the flow once class starts.

Manny eyes me with a smirk as I lie on my mat.

"Wild night?" he jokes.

"He came over last night!" I hiss, leaning over so he hears me clearly.

"Bar boy?" Manny gasps, grinning ear to ear.

"This is your fault for bailing on me."

"I'll keep bailing on you if it gets you to sleep with bar boy."

"You are unbelievable." I get into child's pose as class begins. "And stop calling him that."

"You would have taken him home at some point," Manny says.

My mouth drops open. "I resent that!" I whisper.

"Am I wrong?" He lifts an eyebrow.

"Screw you." God, he's probably not wrong.

Adriana gives us a stern look, gently moving us to the next pose.

"Focus on your downward dog," Manny says.

"Focus on *your* downward dog!" I counter, hips up, ass in the air.

"I bet you were downward dog last night," he mumbles with a snort.

I don't respond, instead pin him with a stare. He cackles, which summons another look from the instructor.

"What is this? *Sleeping with the Enemy*?" he jokes.

"Pretty sure that was about an abusive stalker."

"Getting it out of your systems because the tension was off

the fucking charts?"

Christ, was it that obvious? "Sure, we'll go with that."

"Whatever it is, I am fucking thrilled about it. Somebody had to take one for the team," he says, and we're both starting to sweat.

"I didn't take one for the team. Don't make him sound like a piece of meat."

"Well, either way, now you can move on."

"Yeah," I say quickly, automatically.

But can I? Or do I want to do it again and again?

"Oh shit," he says.

"What?" I'm in warrior pose, trying to keep my balance in this conversation. The sweat is dripping down my face.

"I know that look," he whispers.

"What look?"

"You like him!" His eyes widen with enthusiasm.

"Absolutely not." Warrior one pose to warrior two, and I'm barely keeping it together.

"Well, you don't hate him."

"Maybe I do." I'm tempted to stomp my foot.

"So, you're hate fucking? That's hot."

I grunt and huff something unintelligible. At this point, I don't have it in me to argue.

"And it was so good, wasn't it?" He giggles.

"It was *so* good," I groan, almost embarrassed to even be saying it.

"Agostina!" Adriana sternly calls out in the middle of class.

"Dammit," I grumble. "I hate when she uses my full name."

***

I slept with one coworker once and vowed to never do it again. We've all succumbed to a shitty line cook — just ask Alexis. But now, I don't fuck coworkers. I don't muddle the two, and I don't know what the hell I'm doing. Honestly, probably assuming he'll be out of here soon enough. That I'll get handed the position and he'll leave.

The one time I did sleep with a coworker, he spent the next couple of shifts following me around like a lost puppy, hoping for a touch, an acknowledgment. Something. I hated it.

It was a mess.

I get ready for the inevitable awkwardness, the disaster I have brought upon myself. I'll ignore him the best that I can—while working the bar together, fucking hell—and we'll get through the shift just fine. I can do this.

But when I step behind the bar, he just gives a simple, "Hey." He doesn't even look at me.

I walk around to make sure everything is stocked and prepped for tonight, and he moves to the side to stay out of my way. He's playing this part just how I need him to. He's well aware of what this is and he's not clamoring for anymore. He's doing what I asked.

And surprise, surprise, I hate this, too.

Sixteen

GAVIN

I AM HANGING ON by a goddamn thread, pretending to not give a shit, playing the game we always do.

But when I watch her make a drink, I watch her body move—curves I now know, skin I've seen and touched. I move my eyes down to her rib cage, where I bit her soft skin. Is the mark still there? Is she walking around this bar with imprints of my mouth on her body? As she walks to serve guests, I think about her thighs, how they wrapped around me last night.

I know her taste, I know how she feels.

And I know that I need more of it.

"You plan on working today, Gavin?" Trevor asks, laughing, and I quickly snap out of it.

T looks up at me, and her lips curl into a smirk. A playful twist. A realization that I might be under her spell, and now I'm really screwed.

"I'm going to go…get some more stuff." I walk away briskly and take a second to cool off in the walk-in.

Let me just make it to the end of this shift, and then I can go get a beer at the bar and chill out.

I take a deep breath, ready to walk out, when T comes waltzing in. She smiles as she strolls past me to the citrus, smiles as her body grazes by, and then she smiles at me as she walks right out.

Did I mention I'm fucked?

***

"So, I WAS ON my way to a Halloween party last weekend," Alexis says, drink in hand. "And some asshole rear-ended me."

I made it to the end of the shift, crawling to the finish line, and now we've all convened next door as usual.

"Oh shit, are you okay?" Manny asks.

"Ugh, I'm fine. But the guy hauled ass, leaving me with a busted bumper."

The group collectively groans, offering condolences.

"Next thing I know, a cop shows up. So, I'm like okay, maybe he can help me figure out what to do. And then more cops come. A bunch of them, lights and sirens. So now I start freaking out, like what the hell is going on?"

The table is quietly listening, engrossed in yet another Alexis story.

"Turns out, they thought I was a cop that had just been in an accident, so they called for a bunch of *back up*," Alexis says with flourish as she picks at a mozzarella stick.

"Oh my God, were you dressed like a fucking cop?" T asks wide-eyed with a laugh.

"Officer Baddie, here she is," Manny says.

"I had to step out of the car, in my costume, my ass practically hanging out, and my badge that read Pussy Patrol."

Everybody breaks into raucous laughter.

"You deserve a drink for that one," Manny says.

"I was literally about to shit my pants."

T is laughing with tears in her eyes. "Whose party were you going to anyway?" she asks.

"Some guy I've been talking to. Who did eventually get to see me in my Pussy Patrol outfit, thank you very much."

"The devil works hard, but Alexis works harder." Manny lifts his beer and taps it with hers.

"Remember that year Delfi was the mayonnaise?" Trevor reminisces.

This gets T laughing again. "I do. I entertained her bullshit and I was a hot dog."

"Mayonnaise?" I ask.

"Delfi said if Spirit Halloween could make any costume sexy, she would, too. So she decided she was going to be a sexy jar of mayonnaise," Alexis says.

"It's true," Manny adds. "It was no Pussy Patrol, though."

"But I was just a plain, unsexy hot dog." T shrugs.

"You really could have leaned in with that one," Trevor says.

"Missed opportunity," T agrees.

"I'm sure Camden thought you were sexy," Manny says with a laugh, and I get a weird feeling in my chest.

"Shut up." T shoves him in the shoulder.

"Hellmann's or Duke's?" I ask. "That's the real question."

"Hellmann's," T says with a smirk, looking at me over her glass.

There's danger in that smirk, like playing with fire, but I smile back anyway. A secret game we're playing at this table full of our friends.

"Gavin," Trevor calls out. "Let's play." He motions to the pool table that just emptied out, and I take up the offer to occupy my mind with something else.

"How was your night?" he asks as he reaches for a cue.

"Did I look rough?" I laugh.

"Maybe a little," he says as he breaks the rack. "Sometimes it's tough to get acclimated to the restaurant business. You've been out of it for a bit."

The restaurant, of course. "Right. Yeah. It's been okay, though. Just an off day, I guess." I aim for a corner pocket and miss. You'd think my billiards playing would have gotten better by now.

"I'm here if you need to talk is what I'm saying. We all need to vent, and we're here for each other."

Trevor has been on my side since I started—a friendly face, a trusting coworker. A friend. And I don't miss how lucky I am for that.

"Thanks, Trevor. I really appreciate it."

I buy him a beer and we play another round of pool, falling into conversation about anything and everything. All the while I periodically watch T and the rest of the group have their own long talks filled with loud laughter. This, too, has become a place of comfort for me. Something that finally feels like home.

Trevor and I chime in every now and then, and have our own private conversations, but eventually, we all call it a night.

Agostina makes it home to her place, and I find a way home to mine. I hop into the shower and let the hot water pour down my skin as I think about her. And then I keep thinking about her for the rest of the night.

Seventeen
GAVIN

WHEN I STUMBLE OUT of bed, I find Logan on the couch writing out his dance plan for his private classes.

My brother has been dancing since he was thirteen. Shortly before our parents got divorced, when he didn't want to be home dealing with a house full of fighting adults, he hung out at our neighbor's house instead. And when she went to ballroom dance, he tagged along.

It made him so happy, I could see it immediately. It gave him peace. So, when he almost had to quit because of increased tuition, I made the choice to go to work and pay it for him. Our parents were too busy fighting with each other to care, so I had to. There was no other answer.

And I haven't regretted it a single day since.

Taking care of him in that way was so fulfilling, and I thought if I could set him on that path, he could go do great things away from home. He certainly did, and then I left, too.

I eventually got to work with The Lehman Firm, thinking it could be a way toward my own independence. Logan had started competing, set in his success, and I figured he didn't need me anymore.

My years with the firm were so draining and travel-heavy, but

I assumed I was doing everybody a favor. Logan, me, even my parents.

Now that I've had time to think about all of it, I look back at how much time I spent tied to a job, not able to do anything for myself. Just like Agostina said. Falling in line, falling into a persona—one that sells, one that's professional.

And just like she said, I think about the person I am inside. The one that doesn't care what my parents think—that left a long time ago. The one that aims to be happy, to form real friendships and build real relationships.

I feel a kind of fulfillment I haven't felt in so many years.

I sleepily pad over to the kitchen and grab the box of Cinnamon Toast Crunch, a love leftover from childhood.

"How's work going?" Logan asks.

I yawn as I pour myself a big bowl. "Really good. Well, Steve's a fucking mess." I laugh. "But I'm having a great time. How are the lessons going with Julie?"

"They're going really well," he answers, and a smile follows. His longtime partner Tara is moving away, and he didn't know what he was going to do. He decided to quit competing, which has had him home more, but it's been hard to see him struggle with his career. Probably because I know what it feels like. But tango has been a part of his life for so many years, and it makes me happy to know that he's not giving up just yet. That Julie—whether she knows it or not—is bringing him back to it.

And as I think it, I worry that I know *that* feeling all too well.

"Life surprises you sometimes," I muse with a smile.

"How is it working with her cousin?" he asks, and it jolts me back to the conversation.

"Don't ask," I say immediately.

But my mind just brings me back to last weekend, to being in her house, in her bed. It brings me back to watching her fall apart underneath me.

I think about her talent that leaves me in the dust, her strong voice always aimed at me. I think about her intricate hair that must take hours to do. Who has that kind of time? Her bright eyes, the most mesmerizing blue. Her pink lips, so incredibly soft.

"Not that bad." I smile, and I wonder if my face gives anything away.

Do I look as stupid as he does when he talks about Julie?

I haven't felt this fulfilled in years, and I wonder how much of it is the job and how much of it is her.

My schedule is still unconventional, but much better than how it used to be. And on top of that, Logan and I have been talking again and spending time together. I've missed it.

"Hey," I call out to him as he gathers up his laptop. "I like this. You being home more. Me being home more."

"Me too," he says with a nod.

But with that, he's gone.

Shortly after he leaves, and I down my second bowl of cereal, my phone rings. I grab it quickly, but it's the last person I expect to hear from.

"Hey, mom."

"Hey, hon. How are you?"

"Doing all right," I answer. The last thing I want to do is have a long, drawn-out conversation, but I try to stay positive.

"How's work been? Traveling anywhere new?"

I haven't told my parents about the layoff. To be fair, I haven't talked to either of them in at least a month, and it didn't seem like information I needed to let them know. I used to send them money on occasion, but it's been a while. Maybe that's what she's calling for.

"Actually, mom," I start. "I got laid off."

"What do you mean?"

"The company had some layoffs, and I was part of it," I say. "But it's okay. I started a new job."

"What about Logan?"

"He's still dancing. We're doing okay."

"Well." She sounds a bit concerned. "You think you guys will make it up for the holidays, then?"

"I'm not sure."

"I can make some nice turkey. Potatoes," she pushes. "I know you guys love my green bean casserole. Have you talked to your father?"

I run a hand down my face. This is exactly what I didn't want. "No, I haven't."

After the divorce, my mother dated plenty. And as for my father, he eventually remarried a couple of years back.

"Well, of course not. He always was too busy for everything involving his family, wasn't he?"

That might be my cue to go. "I can call him later. I'm not sure about the holidays this year, mom."

Logan and I don't fly back home too often. Our parents still live in Pennsylvania, still hate each other, and still bug us to come visit during holidays. I built up a lot of points with my old job, which helped with airfare, but sometimes scheduling was difficult.

And now working in the restaurant, my schedule might be even more complicated. We've got holiday parties booked, busy weeks ahead. And, I realize, when it comes to the holidays, I would much rather spend it with The Ivy crew than my parents.

"Let me know, then. Maybe I'll go visit. I could use a nice little vacation, go hang out at the beach."

That sounds even less appealing.

"Sure, mom."

"Okay well, love you honey."

"Love you, too," I say automatically then hang up the phone.

***

I WIPE DOWN THE bar top with a towel, cleaning up as I go, wrapping up the night.

"Who wants to hit up the Alley Cat tonight instead?" Manny asks.

"I'm down," Trevor responds.

"Yeah, let's do that. Derek's working," T responds.

I don't know what the Alley Cat is, but now it's a habit I've fallen into. Following where they go after work, enjoying their company, spending time with everybody. And if T happens to go, it's certainly a bonus.

"Sure." I shrug. "I'll text my brother."

This bar isn't a common hangout—the Knotty Bar is still the most convenient location—but this one is a little wilder:

dimmed lights, neon signs, loud music, and a makeshift dance floor. And some of the bartenders have familiar faces. Like Derek, clearly.

Our big group makes its way to some tables and barstools near a corner. I catch Logan come in, Julie by his side, and briefly wonder if he realizes T will be here, too.

"Hey," he says once he's come up to me. "We were in class, so I brought Julie."

"You're doing field trips now?" I tease.

He laughs in response, but he might be blushing. "We'll be over there, alright?"

I give Julie a wave, and he heads back to their table, but it doesn't take long for Julie to cast her eyes on T. And for T to notice, too.

She grabs my arm and squeezes, letting out an uncharacteristic gasp. "What the hell is my cousin doing here with your brother?"

Logan and Julie are sitting quietly in a corner, talking amongst themselves, and I can't lie that it looks at least *a little* involved. She doesn't wait for an answer, anyway, just walks over to them and stands in front of their table.

"Julieta!" I hear from where I'm at. "What the fuck?"

Logan looks mostly terrified, while Julie just looks over it. What I know about Julie is only what I've pieced together from Logan or her visits to the restaurant. She's a lawyer, she's overworked, and she rarely gets out. Though judging by this surprise encounter, and the fact that she signed up for private dance classes with him, I'd say she's trying to get out more.

Maybe we're all working through our own reinventions.

"A last-minute plan?" T asks, her jaw open.

Well, that answers that, I guess.

The conversation ends soon enough with smiles and laughs, and T comes back to our table.

"My cousin out on a weeknight? With your brother?" She eyes me suspiciously. "You know anything about that?"

I shake my head no. I'm not going to get into the middle of it. But then she heads over to the bar and leans across it like she always does, asking Derek for whatever she wants.

He lines up shot glasses, mixes up who knows what, and pours. Derek places them on a tray, and she gives him a wink as she turns to carry it right to Julie and Logan's table.

"What the hell is this?" Julie asks, sniffing the liquor suspiciously.

T hands them out, passing some to Manny and me, surprisingly.

"Chuck Norris," she says over the growing crowds in the bar, and Manny gives me a look. "Cheers losers!"

We shoot it back and almost immediately wince. What the hell is that?

"Jesus, is that hot sauce?" Julie makes a face as she slams the glass down.

"That was awful," T agrees. "So, Gavin's brother. We meet again."

I chuckle as I grab the shot glasses to bring back up to the bar. Logan can be on the receiving end of her interrogation now. But suddenly, the music gets louder and poppier, the DJ really getting into it.

"See you on the dance floor!" T calls out, and I can't help

but smile. Always the life of the party.

And Julie, like everybody else under her spell, follows her right out to that floor.

Agostina starts to hop and sway, moving her hands from side to side. I can't keep up with the movement as I watch, and I shouldn't even be trying.

Except I can't help myself. I sneak onto the dance floor and move over to her.

"Are you okay? I saw your arms flailing around and thought you were calling out for help," I joke, pushing her buttons to get a reaction.

"Get fucked, Gavin!" she shouts over the music but smiles as she shimmies away.

Dammit, I like her.

I find Logan at his table, so I walk over. He keeps his eyes on Julie, and I keep my own on Agostina.

She's in the middle of the dance floor, hips swaying to the steady beat. There's nothing silly about her dancing. Not at all. Not as I watch her body move, as my eyes scan her skin and curves. She's in those barely functioning flip-flops, a tank top she wears under her work uniform. Her braid is loose and coming undone, her hair falling around her face. I know what that hair looks like out of its braid, when it's spread out against her bedsheets. I should probably look away, but I pinpoint all the places I kissed. All the places my hands touched. She's flushed from dancing, a pretty pink hue I've seen everywhere. Christ. It's taking unbearable effort to keep from touching her again.

She notices me staring and lifts an eyebrow like I've been caught, but I don't break it. I hold it defiantly.

"Ah, shit," Logan mumbles.

"What?"

"You slept with her, didn't you?"

Maybe I should look embarrassed, I don't know, but when it comes to her, my face doesn't do anything but smile. I don't give him an answer—I'm sure the blush I'm trying to hide is answer enough. I finish the last sip of my beer just as Julie leaves the dance floor, making her way right to Logan.

Agostina takes a break from dancing shortly after, too, walking past me to get back to the bar. As she does, her body grazes mine, shoulder to my chest. It's the closest we've been all week, and I wish I could grab her and hold her there.

Did I say just once was fine for me? I lied.

When she reaches the bar, a man makes his way over to her immediately. He stands too close to her, talks loudly in her ear, and the look on her face screams discomfort. She takes some steps back, and I walk in that direction without thinking and set my hands on the bar, a wall between her and the asshole talking to her. She'll probably fucking kill me for this later.

"Can I help you?" the man asks me, annoyed.

"Get lost," I say. I absolutely have a death wish right now.

"Excuse me?"

"He said get fucking lost," T says loudly, staring him down.

"You don't have to be so rude," he says, offended.

"And you don't have to be so annoying. I already said no."

"Bitch," he spits out as he walks away.

But she continues to look unbothered.

"Fucking loser." She rolls her eyes. "Derek, some more shots, please. And make them good this time."

I know that she can take care of herself, I do, but I want to do it, too. And that might be a lot to think about right now. Luckily, I don't have to when she grabs a tray of new shots and is already on the move.

"Let's go," she says loudly above the noise, and I undoubtedly follow as she carries the tray to the table with Logan and Julie.

They seem to be having a serious conversation, one that T doesn't register, because she sets the tray down with flourish and yells, "Panty Dropper!"

"Seriously, how is your liver okay?" Julie asks.

"Better not to ask," T says. "Besides we're celebrating you leaving your house for once."

Manny and I take shots from the tray, and at this point, I'm wondering if *my* liver is going to be okay.

"You're fucking hilarious," Julie deadpans.

"I know. To being hilarious," T toasts.

"And panty droppers," Manny adds, not referring to the drink.

"And panty droppers!" she repeats, eyeing me over the rim of the glass.

I down the shot in an instant, this one much better than the first, coping with whatever I have to tonight. But I'm starting to wonder if just once was enough for her, too.

"I need to go home," Julie says, words slurred.

T jumps into action just as she does. "Logan, can you take her home?"

Julie insists she's fine, insists that Logan stay and hang out, and T just laughs.

"I've got her," Logan says as he gently helps walk her out. "I'll see you back home, okay?" he says to me.

I nod, waving goodbye as they head outside.

The night winds down quickly after that, everybody dispersing and making their own plans to get home.

My phone lights up with a text from Logan, asking if T could get Julie's car from the dance studio.

"Hey, can you get Julie's car?" I ask.

"Yeah, already on it," T says. "I took her car keys while she was dancing."

"Always one step ahead, huh?" I smile. "She parked it at the dance studio."

"The dance studio?"

Did I just stick my foot in my mouth?

"Must have been where they met up and he drove," I say with a shrug, playing it cool.

Most of our group is leaving—Trevor has an early guitar lesson, Chad is working the lunch shift, and Jordan gets up early for the gym as it is. But Manny is deep in conversation with somebody he met tonight, and Alexis is chatting with Derek.

The liquor is getting to me, and suddenly, I want to dance. I want to be out on that floor as carefree as her. So, I walk over and move to the music. I'm not a great dancer, not like Logan anyway, but I think I do okay.

At least okay enough that T looks at me, lips curling into an amused grin, and then comes over and joins me.

Our dance is not coordinated, not smooth. It's a jumble of arms and legs, shoulders and hips. But it's freeing and ridiculous and fun. She doesn't give a shit what anybody thinks, and I try it on for size, too. The alcohol is helping, facilitating this night that's slightly out of character for me.

The neon lights are brighter, and the music is poppier, and Agostina is so joyous in how she dances, in how she lives.

But then the DJ starts to wind down, playing songs that are slower and moodier. It doesn't stop her, though, it just has her moving closer. We sway to the beat, hips moving closer and closer until we're flush. Her arms drape loosely over my shoulders, and I hold on to her waist for some stability.

"You're not a terrible dancer," she says.

"You've got to stop throwing out these compliments. I can only handle so much."

And she laughs. That musical, jovial laugh I love to hear.

My arms wrap around her back, pulling her close to me. Her arms aren't loose anymore. They're firm around my neck as we sway slowly, not even following the beat. Our foreheads touch, and the bartender announces last call.

Bathed in neon lights, our faces are inches apart as she stares at my mouth. She could fucking devour me with that look. But I smell the alcohol on her breath, and she must smell it on mine, too. My body is nothing but heat and ache for her, but we're both too drunk for this.

"This isn't a good idea," I whisper. We've all had too much.

She drops her arms quickly, and I wonder if I imagine the look of hurt on her face.

"Right. Let's get a car," she says, all business. "We can share with Manny and Alexis."

We fall back into our lanes, a reminder that this was just a night of dancing and the sex was only once.

"Okay," I say with a nod, but I want her touch again. I want the closeness. And I think I messed up.

When the driver pulls up to her apartment first, she unbuckles her seatbelt and squeezes Manny's cheeks with a soft smile. "See you all tomorrow," she says, her words running into each other. "Text me when you get home, please."

"Love you, rubia." Manny gives her a quick kiss on the cheek.

"Will do," Alexis says, wrapping her arms around T in a big hug.

"Thanks for the dance," I stupidly add in, and Manny and Alexis look right at me.

"Sure," T responds, but the tone might as well mean go fuck yourself.

With that, she steps out, and we have the driver wait until she's made it inside to take us home.

"Oh boy," Manny mumbles.

I shake my head once, a *let's not talk about this now,* whatever the hell *this* is, and they respect it. Alexis links arms with us both, and we stay quiet, and sleepy, the whole ride home.

Eighteen
AGOSTINA

I'm dragging today. Hell, most of us are. Manny and I were awake early enough for yoga, downing some aspirin and energy drinks, and I managed to get both mine and Julie's cars, but everything is catching up to me now. I can't believe I'm saying this, but I might be getting too old for this shit.

Gavin and I have been tiptoeing around each other after our quick goodbye last night. We said it was one time. I made the fucking rule. But I was feeling too much after those stupid fucking shots, and the dark bar, and his body dancing against mine. And I guess I didn't expect him to actually follow it.

I catch a guest walking up to the bar and recognize him immediately.

"Hey, Camden." I give him my best server smile. "How are you?"

"Better now that I see you." He thinks he's charming, but I can play along.

My answering laugh is polite. "What can I get you?"

"I'll take the usual," he says. "Haven't seen you in a while."

"Yeah. I've been busy."

"I'm going to a party tonight. Want to come?"

As I turn around to grab a bottle of beer, I run right into

Gavin. "Behind," I say with emphasis.

I pass Camden the beer. "Where at?"

Camden used to be a line cook at The Ivy, and yeah, I was attracted to him. When we were at the bar one night, he was sloshed and pulling his car keys out of his pocket. I stopped him right there, offering to take him home instead. I heard more than a couple of murmurs from the group, as they love to get into anybody's business. But when I took him home, and had my arm around him holding him up as we walked to the door, he turned drunkenly, uncomfortably handsy. And then he kept throwing all this food-related dirty talk at me. Like, *I'm going to stuff my baguette into your hot oven*. And something about a burrito. It was so gross. I quickly said no fucking thank you and drove home.

And honestly, it was probably better that way. 'Cause whatever man is referring to my body as a hot oven probably couldn't find my clit anyway.

But in the moment people wanted to believe what they wanted to. And they want to talk whatever shit they want to. And sometimes it's just easier to let them.

Maybe I should care about the rumors involving Camden and me, but the ones closest to me, the friends that matter, know the truth.

Camden quit a couple of weeks later anyway. He left to go work at a steakhouse some miles away, but it's not uncommon to find him visiting from time to time.

I have no interest in going to this party, but I can be friendly.

And—while I recognize that I can be a pain in the ass—maybe it can piss Gavin off for a moment. Right now, all I care about is getting a reaction.

"Somebody got an Airbnb on the beach," he says.

"Oh." I nod. "Cool."

It might be trickier than I thought to feign interest.

Two women sit at the bar near him, and I move to greet them.

"Good evening, ladies. What can I get started for you?"

"Actually, we're here for him." They point to Gavin, and I answer with a tight smile.

Of course, they are.

"So good to see you again," he says in his charming voice.

He gets them drinks, he openly flirts. They order food, and their tits are practically falling out of their shirts. I'm not even mad about it. Those are cute fucking shirts. Good for them.

When I turn to grab another beer for Camden, Gavin comes close.

"So. Camden," he says quietly. Kind of a joke, but prying.

I don't say anything. I don't feel like it.

"Not that it's my business," he adds.

"It's not," I respond curtly.

I take the beer to Camden with a smile.

The bar fills quickly, crowds gathering as we get into our busy hours. Gavin and I continue to move throughout the bar like we're fighting for space. Trevor just aims to stay out of our way.

I serve an espresso martini; Gavin counters and serves two.

When the printer goes off, we rush to get tickets and fight to serve customers. I move quickly through the bar, grabbing bottles, handling glasses, and scooping ice. He greets everybody with a big smile on his face.

I spy my regulars walking in. In the time he's been here, he's gotten some, too, including the one that asked for him when she sat down.

"I need a New River IPA, please," I call out to Trevor.

"Make that two," Gavin says, moving through the bar with purpose.

Carol needs her glass of red with cup of ice on the side. He handles Penny's Bloody Mary, serving her with a wink.

I lean over to chat with Camden some more. I laugh with Jenny as I hand over her Bacardi and diet. He jokes with his guests, too, laughing loudly and carrying on.

When he picks up a tab, he holds it up to me. "Looks like we both have plans tonight, T." There's a phone number scribbled on the bottom.

"Sounds like fun," I say, giving him my most unbothered smile.

By the end of the night, we're all sweating. Well, except Trevor, who just looks like he doesn't know what the hell is going on with us. I don't know either. Maybe some days I can be a bitch and a brat.

And maybe most days I don't care.

"Who needs a drink?" he asks, lifting his own hand up.

I lift both of mine in the air.

"Let's clean up and get out of here, then," he says.

He works on the tip outs, and Gavin and I get busy restocking everything.

"Move," I say, walking through the bar as I organize for tomorrow morning's shift.

We fight for bottles, fight for space. Like the tension has built up and come back tenfold, a building electricity between us. I stare him down, willing him to melt.

"You move," he throws back, and I consider ripping him a new asshole.

"We need to restock the wine bottles," I say, moving in the direction of the closet.

"I can grab them," Gavin offers.

"No, I've got it."

But when I rush into the closet and reach for the bottles of wine we're out of, he quickly follows and shuts the door behind us.

Nineteen
GAVIN

"Wнат тне неLL is your problem?" I ask.

Agostina puts her hands on her hips. "I don't have a problem, what's yours?"

"This is so stupid, how are we here again?"

"You're welcome to leave if working with me is making you too uncomfortable."

I can't help the laugh that comes out of my mouth. "I'm not going anywhere."

"Well, I've got a party to go to tonight, so can you move out of the way?"

"Sure. I've got to call up that guest at the bar. See what she wants to do tonight."

"Have fun, then."

"Oh, I will," I throw back.

"Great," she says loudly, stepping toward me.

"Great," I repeat, getting closer.

Our breaths are in sync; our eyes are in a heated stare. Words are flying back and forth in an angry volley, the game we always play turned up to one hundred.

"What the hell are we doing, T?" I ask, resigned, and I feel the heat coming off her body. I would let it swallow me whole without second thought.

Her eyes briefly move to my mouth, and I want to throw everything out the window.

"I don't want to go out with her," I admit. "And I know you don't want to go to that fucking party with some loser named Camden."

"You don't fucking know that," she argues.

"And let's forget about the fucking Alley Cat."

I really need to not fuck this up. I'm trying my damn hardest right now.

"Take your mask off," I whisper harshly, inches away from her.

"Take yours off first," she counters angrily.

There's always a dizzying push and pull between us, a constant fight with what we should or shouldn't be doing. I don't even know what's right anymore, but suddenly, I'm taking after her—going for what I want, making no apologies for it.

Like a gravitational pull, I grab her hips, and my mouth crashes into hers. She kisses me back roughly before breaking it.

"You make me want to scream," she says, pulling at my tie.

"My name?"

"You're talking too much again."

"Tell me you want this again," I plead. "Tell me you want this like I do."

"Thought we decided just once to get it out of our systems," she says with bite.

"I don't think either of us believed that."

"Don't tell me what I believe." She pulls at my tie again, jolting me forward.

I brace my hands against the door, bracketing her body in. I don't know what it is about being near her that drives me so wild. "Maybe I don't want you out of my system just yet," I admit. "Maybe just once wasn't enough."

"Not for you, it seems."

Not even a little bit, not with how much I crave your touch, I want to tell her.

"How about once more, then?" I say instead. My lips dance along her neck.

"*Now* you think that's a good idea?"

I don't know what's a good or bad idea right now. "Sure. We're both adults here."

She lifts an eyebrow. "Is this you being persuasive?"

"Is it working?"

"Not sure yet."

I bend down and pick her up with ease. Her legs immediately wrap around me as I push her against the door. My mouth meets her throat; her hands pull at my hair. Not sure what it says about me that this is the most exciting, electrifying connection I've ever had.

Every touch feels like lightning with her. Every kiss feels like I could drown in it.

I press my lips to hers, kissing her feverishly as she moves her hips against me, as she quietly sighs against my mouth. Biting my lip, seeking out my tongue. I swallow back a groan, gripping her thighs as we move. This feels like a fever dream.

"Is it working now?" My voice is sandpaper.

"Maybe a little," she pants, her own voice rough with need.

She grinds against me as I kiss along her jaw, as I feel the delicious warmth between her legs.

"Nobody finds out about this," she warns, and I almost choke.

"Who would I tell?"

"Your big fucking mouth would tell Trevor, for starters."

"You would tell Manny," I argue. "And Alexis."

"This stays between us," she says, not exactly denying that she probably would tell them.

I nod, practically in disbelief that she's agreeing to this again. "Just you and me."

She reaches for the doorknob beneath her and locks it. "What the hell are we doing, Gavin?"

I hold her legs around my waist, moving against her, and she closes her eyes. I don't know what the hell we're doing, just that it feels explosive. Just that I hardly recognize myself and these wild feelings.

"Having fun, right?" I groan. "Or do you mean why are we such horny teenagers around each other?"

I press my lips to the side of her throat, leaving a trail of messy kisses. Our movements become rougher, and I don't know what to do or how to stop. Now I'm determined to get her there.

She moans in my ear, her legs starting to shake.

"You've got to be quiet, baby," I whisper.

"You shut up," she counters then kisses me. "This is such a bad idea," she breathes out.

"You like bad ideas." My voice trembles with need as I'm barely hanging on, as I tilt her hips and grind against her.

Then her body gently shakes as her eyes go wide and she gasps. "Fuck."

"Yeah?" I might be just as surprised as she is, watching as she unravels, holding her close right against the door. "That's it."

I kiss her as she comes down, struggling to process everything. I need a minute in the walk-in. Christ, what is the deal with this fucking closet?

I set her down gently, making sure she's stable, and then I lean against the door myself. I'm out of breath, pulled apart. I'm used to feeling so in control. Precise and pragmatic. But she's making me lose every bit of it, one shift at a time. One day, one touch, one kiss at a time.

Suddenly I'm the type of guy who bites and licks and begs. Who dry humps in closets. I'm now the type who is flirty and messy and desperate to fuck her again.

She runs her fingers through her hair and adjusts her vest and tie. Mask back on, back to business. Her hands still shake, and I want to grab them, but I know she'd pull away. I take a deep breath and fix what feels like my never-ending hard-on for her.

I run a hand down my face and clear my throat. "How are we playing this? You go out first?"

I can almost see when she comes back to it, when she realizes where we are and what's happened and what nonsense we fall into when we're together.

She reaches for the bottle of wine she came in for, and I try to throw the act back on. The salesman, the friendly professional. The one that knows this is just for fun.

All of this is just for fun. Honestly, the most fun I've had.

"I still don't like you," she says, nowhere near as aggressive as I know she can be.

I smile. "Of course not. I don't like you either."

And with that, she walks out.

Twenty

AGOSTINA

"YOU LOOK LIKE HELL," Trevor says when I make it back to the bar.

"Aw, thanks." But my body is on edge. You'd think it wouldn't be, considering I just fucking came in the storage closet, but I'm shaky and uneasy. A certified mess.

And when I see Gavin walking back to the bar with an easy smile, the swoop in my belly grows bigger.

Don't think about it. Don't think about the loneliness that crawls in, the quiet that can be suffocating. Don't think about the need to have somebody in my too-empty house, in my too-empty bed. Don't think about my cold sheets and the desire for a warm body to occupy it.

But this isn't that, a small voice pops up to argue. It's the desire for *his* warm body, not just any one.

I want him in my bed again.

"Are we just about done?" I ask.

"Yeah, think so," Trevor answers. "Next door?"

"Not tonight." I shake my head. "I'm tired."

"What about you, Gavin?" Trevor asks.

"I don't think so. I'm pretty tired, too," he says.

We're avoiding any eye contact, but Trevor looks between

us suspiciously as we head out to the parking lot together. It's almost midnight, and I am wired.

"Alright, then. See you tomorrow. Make good choices, T," he says with a smirk.

"I always do."

As he drives away, I turn to Gavin, who's getting into his own car.

"Coming over?" I ask.

He gives me a smug smile in return, a dictionary equivalent of bad choices, and says, "Yeah, I'm coming over."

***

WHEN I WALK INTO my house, I move backward, pulling my work shirt off me and throwing it on the floor. He follows, unbuttoning his vest and loosening his tie with a smile on his face.

I reach for him without thought, my hands going for what they want right in the moment, and kiss him desperately.

"Just once more, then?" he says in between kisses.

"Something like that." I grab his shirt with my fists.

He hums. "I could do this forever."

"Forever isn't on the table," I correct him. This isn't a thing. I don't even know what this is. He'll be temporary enough, just like the rest of them. This is all surface level, as it should be.

"Then I guess I better soak up all I can get."

I place my palm on his chest. "When this is over, it's over, Gavin," I warn.

"Ooh, I love when you say my name so angrily." He bites at my shoulder, hands spanning my back, holding me so close.

"You're such a pain in my ass."

He laughs softly then gets serious. "When is it over, T-rex?"

"I don't know yet," I grumble. I don't know anything right now, just that I dry humped this asshole in the storage closet and now he's in my house again and I want to keep dry humping him because I'm a disaster.

"Okay. You tell me when, T. You call the shots."

"I always call the shots."

"Oh, I know." He smirks as he leans down to plant one soft kiss on my collarbone.

"We do this until I get lead bartender. Then you can quit."

He takes a step back. "But if I quit, who are you going to yell at?"

"I'm sure I'll find somebody." I pull on his shirt to bring him toward me again.

"And if I get lead bartender?" he asks, teasing.

"Then it's more reason for me to yell at you," I say. "And we keep this a fucking secret."

He kisses me like an agreement, moving past shaking hands, and sleeping with a coworker instead. It's fiery and passionate and rough—everything I love about his mouth.

"You know what I thought about? What I wondered?" he asks in my ear, pulling me in almost impossibly closer.

"What's that?"

"If you walked around all night with that hickey on your body. If my bite was still on your skin, underneath your clothes. I wanted to know."

"Did you?"

"I really did."

I lift my tank top above my head and throw it across the room, giving him access to the spot right along my ribcage. The mark has faded, a barely visible circle from its originally bright color.

He touches it gently, running his fingers up and down my skin. "Guess I need to do it again."

"Guess we're doing all of it again, aren't we?"

He just chuckles, a low rumble I feel everywhere.

"This is trouble, bar boy," I warn.

"I like trouble." He unbuttons his work shirt and slides it off his arms. I watch, mesmerized by the most basic movements like an idiot. Why does he make everything look so *good*?

This is just sex, I need to remind myself. Great fucking sex, but still. Just sex. What's a couple of orgasms between coworkers?

Except for the minor detail that he's also trying to take the job I want.

This is definitely trouble. And just like he claims, I like trouble, too.

I reach for his pants to unbuckle his belt, but he picks me up and throws me over his shoulder, walking us to my room.

He tosses me on the bed and crawls over, placing his hands on either side of my head.

"I don't exactly make a habit out of dry humping in storage closets," he says then kisses me.

"Good to know."

He sits up and pulls the bottom half of my clothes off swiftly, and my body is vibrating with anticipation. The closet was a precursor to this, delicious in its own right, but could never compare.

"This is so much better," he whispers against my belly button. "Not that dry humping in closets isn't fun. I'll do that whenever you want, T-bone," he says with a smirk as his hands grip my thighs. His fingers press gently into my flesh, indents on my skin. I hope he leaves a mark there, too.

"You're an idiot," I huff, but it's quickly followed by a soft moan as his fingers reach between my legs.

"Baby, you're soaked," he says gruffly.

"If you call me baby one more fucking time," I manage between a groan.

"Did you miss me?" he asks, kissing along my thighs.

"Sounds like *you* missed me." I grab the back of his head.

"You have no fucking idea," he says with that rasp in his voice.

Barely hanging on by thread, that's how I want him. But it's starting to feel like I'm the one barely getting by.

I weave my fingers through his hair, pull his head up, and point to my inner thigh. "Here."

He gives me a devilish smile as he obliges and leans down to gently bite my skin. His lips suck at my thigh, rough suction that makes me desperate, and leave a bright spot behind.

"Where else?" His voice is deep, jagged.

I motion to my waist, more skin for him to sink his teeth into. He hums in appreciation as he does it, the vibrations echoing against my body, and looks up at me with a smile.

"And here," I say, my own fingers between my legs, soothing

the ache.

His eyes are dark as he watches me. He grabs my wrist and moves my fingers to his mouth, sucking gently. Then his mouth makes contact, his tongue laps at my wetness, and it makes me goddamn weak. *Fuck*, I missed this, too. I lift my leg and position it over his shoulder, wrapping myself around him, pulling him in closer. Keeping him where I want him.

His mouth on me is dangerous. Unrelenting and passionate. He alternates between soft kisses and long, thorough licks. There's suction, too, drawing every bit of pleasure out of me until I'm writhing and whimpering. He's not shy about any of it, digging his fingers deeper into my thighs, holding them open.

And I'm not shy about craving it, screaming for it, and falling apart under his mouth.

"Yeah, you missed me." He sighs as he leans back on his heels and smiles at me. My eyes follow the curves of it, the twist of it, the unbridled joy. God, that stupid smile. I think I like it.

I think I like it so much.

We do this until I get lead bartender, I remind myself.

I see him reach over and open the drawer to my nightstand, pulling out a condom.

My leg is still positioned over his shoulder, and he keeps it there as he slides in, watching where we meet. He moans softly as his hands circle my waist.

"Fuck, it's so good between us, isn't it?" he breathes out.

I don't have it in me to answer, so I nod.

And as he thrusts in harder, I study the muscles in his arms, the tattoo that moves as his body does. I study his sharp jaw, tracing it slowly with my fingertips. My eyes scan every inch of hot skin, and I feel like I'm on fire, too.

This feeling is like uncontrollable lust. Desperate and demanding, there's no other word. I need his body next to mine for clarity and calmness. I want skin to skin.

I bring him down to me and kiss him roughly. "Please," I beg.

"Please, what?" he smirks.

Please, anything.

"Let me guess." He kisses me. "Please, don't stop." He thrusts in a little deeper. "Please, harder," he groans, his own words seemingly affecting him. "Please, Gavin, make me come."

I'm practically panting, my mouth against his shoulder as I bite it.

"I can do that," he smirks. "Can't I?"

"I don't know, can you?" I fight back.

"I'm so good at it, aren't I?" he goads, kissing my neck.

"Your ego is feeling a little desperate today, huh?" I manage, the words coming out strained, much less bite than they usually have.

"You can tell me," he eggs on, whispering against my ear. "You can tell me how good I am at making you come."

This is a kind of playful I can handle. Something that ends once the sex is over and he's out of my house. And he is good at making me come. So fucking good at it as he hits that perfect spot and I float higher and higher until I burst like a balloon.

"Oh fuck," I moan, gripping his arms, digging my nails into them.

"Just like that," he says in a low tone, watching me intensely as I crash down.

Except when I come, shaking against his body, all I feel are pieces of him conforming to mine. A sort of longing I've never felt before, where I want to prolong this for as long as I can. Where I don't want it to end when everything else does.

His own release is imminent as he tucks his face into the side of my neck and groans deliciously into my skin.

"Fuck, what are you doing to me?" he pleads, catching his breath, and I almost wonder that myself.

I lie against his body, uncomfortably unsatisfied, this unrelenting feeling continuing to build. So, I take his face in my hands and chase what I know. And I beg one more time.

"Please," I ask quietly. "Make me come again."

Twenty-One
GAVIN

"Can't get enough, baby?" I murmur against her skin, breathing in her scent.

But I'll do whatever she asks. I'd do anything for her, gladly.

I move her body so her back is flush with my front, and then I twist us around to face the mirror positioned in the corner of her room.

There's the naked reflection of her against the backdrop of me. She kneels, positioning her knees wider apart, letting me see all of her. Her hair is out of its usual braid, cascading down her back and in messy swirls framing her face.

I kiss her shoulder, something messy and passionate. Open mouth kisses along her soft skin.

She stretches her arm to wrap around the back of my neck. My own hand starts at the base of her throat and then trails lower.

"You're so beautiful," I whisper.

She watches my hand glide across her skin, and I can feel her anticipation. Her heartbeat, her rapid breathing. It's a wild thing, enveloping us both.

"You're shaking." My breath is on the shell of her ear. "You're so needy."

She probably hates that I say it, giving me a hard stare in the mirror.

But I just smile as my fingers work their way into her, slick and warm.

She closes her eyes, letting her head fall back, but my other hand grips her chin. "No. Open them, look at you."

She studies our reflection, and I can't look away myself. Not from her gorgeous body on display, not from her luscious mouth falling open. She grips my forearm, and I welcome her touch enthusiastically.

And when I catch her piercing eyes in the mirror, I whisper, "Maybe I'm the needy one."

My fingers dip in and out, and her body vibrates with desperation.

"Maybe I can't get enough of you," I admit as I work in messy, erratic circles.

Our bodies make dancing shadows against the wall, barely recognizable, secretive like the rest of this. But when I look at our reflection, and I see both of us so clearly, it's damning evidence.

Our moves are becoming stilted, chaotic, like we're both losing complete control.

My teeth graze below her ear, and she moans. My free hand slides up to pinch her nipple, and I wish I could swallow up all of her gorgeous sounds.

"Keep going," she whimpers, and I'm so goddamn turned on.

"I want you so fucking much," I grind out, unable to stop talking. "My hands want to do nothing else but touch you."

And that's the truth. I crave her—touch and smell and taste. But my desire for her stretches beyond the physical. When I see her, my heart jolts. When I'm near her, my heart reaches. And when she says something—*anything*— to me, my fucking heart involuntarily jumps.

I know this is slipping into a messy area, falling into some dangerous territory, but I don't think about it now. Not when she's almost there.

She begged me to make her come again, and I'm beside myself.

I catch her eyes in the mirror, softening.

"Come again for me," I say in her ear. "Let me see you."

And any semblance of control she had left shatters as she comes undone.

She is a fucking marvel to look at as she shakes against me, but I hold her through it, my arms keeping her steady as I kiss everywhere my mouth can reach.

She falls forward on an exhale, resting her elbows on the bed. Her body lifts up, pushing against me as I move behind her.

Does she want more?

"Are you sure?" I quietly ask.

"Yes," she whispers. "Take it."

And I quickly grab another condom before gently sliding in.

"Fuck, baby," I groan, reveling in the unbelievable feel of her.

The rest of me is less than gentle as my fingertips dig into her ribs, as my hips meet hers with every forceful thrust.

I'm too delirious to speak. It feels like an out of body experience as I swim through lust. As I fuck her until my orgasm spills from me, too.

We tumble down onto her bed, shaking and panting.

I feel exhausted. I feel...rearranged.

"Satisfied?" I ask, out of breath.

When I look over at her, I can tell she feels something, too. She looks confused and dazed. And then, between her own heavy breathing, she manages to say the most honest, surprising thing yet.

"I've never felt so goddamn satisfied in my life."

My eyes widen, and my heart swells. "Well, that's a fucking compliment."

I lie still, letting the words soak into my skin, before I make the heavy effort to walk to the bathroom and dispose of the condom. I gently pad my way to the kitchen to grab us a glass of water, and when I make it back, she's laid out on the bed, quietly staring at the ceiling. Gloriously naked, not ashamed of any of it.

I wordlessly pass her the cup.

"Thanks," she mumbles.

I search for my clothes along the floor again. Only the second time, but it feels like it's becoming a common occurrence.

"What's the story behind your tattoo?" she asks as I'm about to throw my shirt back on.

I run a hand along my shoulder. "I got it done years ago. Birthday gift to myself." An impulse decision that my ex didn't care for. "I wanted something kind of fun, loud. Something I could cover up. I liked having this part of me underneath the clothes I wore. A reminder that I was just playing a part."

She hums as she studies the tattoo.

"I kind of forgot about that—the fact that I was playing a

part—and I've been slowly getting back to myself ever since." I finish buttoning my shirt. "Remember when we were talking about dating apps, and you told me not to be myself?"

She lets out a small laugh, and I chuckle in response.

"I know it was a joke, but I started thinking about it. Thing is, I like myself. And I haven't liked myself in a long time. I like the person inside me that's finally seeing light of day again. And it's all because of you."

She furrows her brows. "Why me?"

"I feel like myself with you," I admit. "I don't think I've ever felt like myself with anybody."

She swallows. "You can't say that to me."

"I shouldn't say that to you," I correct, "But I did."

And because I'm already in deep enough, I kiss her. Not quickly, not rushed, but leisurely, softly. Long enough that she's reaching for me again, bringing me down onto the bed. If she asked me to stay, I would without hesitation. I think I would stay forever if she asked.

"See you," she says.

I don't know if she ever will, but I won't worry about that right now.

"I can't wait," I respond.

Twenty-Two
AGOSTINA

"Hola, linda." Javier walks up to the bar and gives me a kiss on the cheek. Sometimes he comes to Sunday brunch, brings his friends, and sips an Aperol spritz on the outdoor patio.

"I have to tell you," he starts, "Julieta is doing amazing."

"At work? I know Babs was giving her a hard time."

"No, no." He shakes his head. "Dancing. You should have seen her at the milonga last night."

I know I didn't hear that correctly. I laugh as I make his cocktail. "The milonga?"

"Claro." He nods. "I haven't seen you out there in a while."

My hand freezes as I pass the drink over to him, my eyebrows lifting in total fucking surprise.

"She was there with a tango instructor," he says.

"Logan?" I practically shout.

"You know him? He's excellent."

Oh, I bet he is.

"And she danced two tandas." He puts two fingers up and gives me a look.

My eyebrows might as well be past my fucking hairline at this point. Milongas are just tango socials where you can go dance all night, but they can still be led by archaic rules such as men have to approach you to dance. And while one dance, or tanda, is sufficient, if he dances two with you, then he is, for lack of a better term, *interested*.

Overworked Julie who never goes anywhere suddenly going to bars and milongas? Damn, I'm proud.

But, also, I'm pissed. Why didn't she say anything?

"Nos vemos, linda," Javier says as leaves me a cash tip and heads to the outdoor tables.

Most of us are wrapping up brunch service, and I'm restocking what I can when Trevor and Gavin come in later for the night shift.

"Hey, T," Trevor says, but I zone in on Gavin instead.

"Your brother is out tango dancing with my cousin, and you didn't think to mention that?" I practically hiss.

"Oh, that makes sense that we saw her at the Alley Cat," Trevor says, butting into the conversation.

We did see her at the fucking Alley Cat on Thursday night. We all opted to go out to the Alley Cat instead of the bar next door for some live music and dancing. And imagine my surprise when I saw Julie with Logan.

God, good for her. She must have hit it off with Logan when she met him at the Knotty Bar weeks ago. And she's going to a milonga in my grandmother's tango shoes, I'm sure.

If only she could see Julie now.

"I'm not at liberty to say," Gavin says, which results in an icy stare from me. "I seem to be holding a lot of secrets these days." He shrugs and throws me a knowing smirk.

I'd punch him if I wasn't so damn involved in this mess. If I wasn't busy fucking the enemy yet again. An avalanche of bad decisions.

I probably could punch him anyway.

He walks around this bar like he knows it now. He moves to see what needs to be restocked. He greets customers with a big friendly salesman smile, upselling like he knows how.

But now I know what his real smile looks like. And how those hands feel when he hits the right spot. I let him leave marks on my skin so I can wear them underneath my clothes.

And I know how he looks when he comes undone, too. I want to see it again and again.

He walks up to me as I'm getting ready to leave. "Later?" he whispers.

"After ten," I tell him. "I have family dinner."

He nods with a smile, but I wonder—and worry—if that smile is just for me.

***

When I walk into tía Maria's house, tía Cecilia is dancing to music playing in the background. The men of the family are gathered outside while the women are moving through the kitchen, prepping for dinner.

Julie must be setting the table, her favorite job where she can usually find some quiet, and I head in that direction.

I pick up some forks and start to help. "You know, it's a surprise how good of a lawyer you are, 'cause you're a shit liar."

"What?" she asks, taken aback.

"Javier came into the restaurant earlier today."

Her face falls.

"And he told me all about how he ran into you at the milonga with *Logan* the *tango instructor*."

Julie's eyes go wide.

"I fucking knew something was up." I set the fork down loudly.

Just then, Delfi steps into the dining room and right into our standoff. "'Kay, the vibe is weird in here."

"Javier told me that you danced two tandas with him," I keep going. "I assumed you were enjoying some sexcapades, but this confirms it."

"Sexcapades?" Julie looks shocked.

"Two tandas?" Delfina is trying to catch up.

But Julie rolls her eyes, shrugging it away, claiming they were just dancing.

"He knows the rules," I add, and I can thank my grandmother for that one.

Julie can't hide it anymore anyway, and armed with this new information, we can't help but smile right at her.

"You *are* dancing!" Delfi says, excited as ever.

But Julie shuts us up, looking to the kitchen to make sure nobody can hear.

"I won't say a word," Delfi adds in. "Though, honestly, I'm a little offended that I wasn't invited."

I can see the storm brewing in Julie's eyes, the build up of guilt and anxiety. And then the clouds part and she starts to cry.

"Shit," I mutter.

We walk over and hug her, willing her to calm down as she

shares her frustrations. As she talks about how she wanted to do something for herself for once.

She's the eldest daughter in the family, taking on more responsibility than she ever should have. Consumed with guilt, unable to have any fun. It's been kind of infuriating to watch.

"Shit, Julie," I say softly. I'm so happy that she's found this outlet, that she's finally going out and living life. And I'm upset that she still feels the need to keep it a secret.

Says the one keeping her own secrets.

"Logan happened to be the instructor when I signed up for the tango classes," she explains, and I can see Delfi's mind working overtime.

"Logan? Like Gavin's brother?" she asks. "Damn, how did I miss that?"

"There's another milonga coming up in a couple of weeks."

"Where is it?" I ask.

Julie rolls her eyes, hesitant to answer.

"Where?" Delfi pushes.

Except what Julie wants is something for herself, and I see it clearly.

"I've got work that night," I hurry to say, and Delfi catches on, excusing herself out of it, too.

Julie smiles in gratitude and continues to set the table, but it seems to be open-ended, like this isn't it, and I've never been shy about prying for information out of her.

"There's more," I say.

She sighs deeply and looks to the kitchen again to make sure nobody can hear. "I signed up to do a competition in San Diego."

My jaw drops. "*Ho-ly shit.*" Julie doesn't leave the state. Julie barely leaves the city she lives in. I was not expecting that, but I guess nothing has been expected these past couple of months. Damn, I really am proud of her. "The San Diego Tango Festival? I saw her there."

My grandmother loved that festival, always claimed it was such a welcoming and loving event. And she was a star every time she appeared.

"God, of course, you did," she says with sigh.

Delfi is beside herself with excitement but quickly reins it in when tía Silvia walks in with platters of milanesas and potato salad, placing them in the center of the table. The rest of the family follows, Leo clearly missing, and we all sit down to eat.

"That is the best thing I've heard all week," Delfina says to me as we carry dirty dishes to the kitchen.

"I'm impressed," I admit.

"We're going, right?"

"Fuck yes, we're going," I say. "We'll sit in the back out of view." What Julie needs right now is support, and we're not going to pass that up.

"You got any fun secrets for me?" she jokes with a giggle.

But just as she asks, tía Maria comes in with my mom and sets her kettle on the stove for mate.

"Hay torta," she says, pulling a chocolate cake out of the fridge.

Delfi's eyes light up, and she reaches for a cake cutter in the drawer. She cuts some slices of cake, plates them, and they all walk out of the kitchen again, those pieces probably going to the men sitting outside chatting.

As they walk out, Cecilia comes in. She pours the last of the wine into her glass and sets the empty bottle aside to be recycled. "Y?" she asks, waiting for some sort of gossip about who knows what.

"Y que?"

"How's it going? How's work?" She leans against the counter.

I sigh, serving myself a slice of the cake. Looks like Publix. "Steve offered the job to somebody else."

"Again?"

"I know, I know." It sounds even worse when she says it. "So, now we're kind of fighting for it."

"Who are you fighting?"

"His name is Gavin. He's Steve's friend." I grab a fork from the drawer and take a bite.

"Is it worth fighting for?"

"I've wanted that job for years, tía. It's not fair."

"You're right." She nods. "But is it worth fighting for?"

I'm reluctant to give her an eye roll, so I just stuff my face with more cake instead.

"For somebody who can't sit still, you sure stick to that place," she says.

"Not you, too."

She laughs. "It's not a bad thing to stay in one place. And it's not a bad thing to move, either. It just comes down to what you want."

"Well, I know what I want."

She sighs. Tía Cecilia and I are the most alike, which is a blessing and a curse most days. It was wonderful when I was younger, able to lean on her for anything, when I could approach her with no judgment. If you ask my mother, she'll tell you I was a wild child who was too stubborn for her own good. That Leo was the easy one, and she just gave up trying to handle me.

Cecilia will still come to my defense. She understands me and gives me grace and patience, but she's not above telling me to get my head out of my ass. Like she's probably about to do.

"Sometimes, we hold on so tightly to our convictions that we forget what we truly want." Her words are gentle, but firm, as she gives me a look. "Are you fighting for the sake of fighting? Are you too stubborn to admit it?"

I give her my biggest scowl. "Whose side are you on anyway?"

"Yours." She smiles. "Always yours."

There's commotion in the kitchen again as my aunts come back in, breaking up our conversation. Maria pours the hot water from the kettle into the thermos.

"Gracias, tía," I say quietly as I frown.

She rubs my arm, a small sign of affection. "Now I'm going to go talk to Julieta."

When I make it home, I get comfortable, throwing on some sweats and a beat up T-shirt. It's a little after ten, and the rhythmic knock on my door is almost like clockwork. I know just who it is.

I won't think about fighting tonight. I won't think about what I may or may not want. Not when it comes to The Ivy anyway. I'll think about this want instead.

I don't even hesitate when I open the door and certainly not when I jump into his arms.

"Hi," he says, smiling from ear to ear.

"Hi."

In a concerning turn of events, my face transforms to mimic his. He closes the door and carries me right to my room.

Twenty-Three
GAVIN

She's lying on her stomach, naked, sprawled out. Sun drenched hair, a golden halo.

She looks softer.

Sam once called her a rigid bitch, and I was so pissed when I heard it. Even when I didn't know her that well, like I do now. I knew then she was not rigid. She's not hard lines, but rounded edges. Soft curves. Beaming warmth once you open her up. And she looks so warm now. She looks inviting and so soft. I run my hands up her thighs slowly, gently, skimming past the hickeys, savoring all of it.

She shifts a little, softly humming. One eye opens. "Hi," she whispers.

I smile. "Hi. Sorry, I couldn't help myself."

She grins in response. "Well, by all means."

And my hands continue their exploration of her.

"You're so gorgeous, T."

Her smile is bashful. Not the smug one she's used to carrying around like armor. This one is vulnerable and shy. Quiet. I love it so much.

It's a little after midnight, and she'll probably kick me out soon, but for now, I'll savor what I can with her.

My hands span her back up to her shoulders and neck where I squeeze and she lightly moans, and then back down grabbing hold of her ass. She tilts her hips upward, her ass meeting my hands, and I spread my fingers wide. My thumbs hook right underneath, and then in between her legs—the warmest, softest spot on her. Her hips tilt again, chasing my thumbs, chasing my hands until soon enough she's up on her knees, and I'm kneeling to put my mouth right on her. Fucking heaven.

I don't tire of her taste, of how she begs for it.

"Fuck, Gav, that's so good."

And when she comes on my tongue, screaming my name into her pillow, I know then I am beyond fucked.

When I get back home, I stroll in, trying not to make any noise and inevitably failing. But it doesn't even matter, because when I step inside, I find Logan and Julie in the kitchen eating what looks like sandwiches de miga, eyes wide like they've just been caught.

"Uh. Hi," I say.

"Oh. Hi," Julie repeats, mid chew.

"This is Julie." Logan jumps in, almost embarrassed. "You've met, right?"

"Uh-huh," I say, biting back a laugh.

"We were just going back to my room," he says, but I'm not letting him off that easy.

"Not so fast." I walk over and pull out a stack of sandwiches. "Thanks." I turn around and walk to my room, leaving them to it, happy to see him happy.

I replay my own memories from tonight, a constant loop in my head of every move, every touch, every sound, and if he hears me whistling like an idiot as I walk away, he doesn't say.

***

"THEY HAD ME WAIT until their cameras were ready so they could film me making a drink."

"I've had guests like that," she says, annoyed. "I hate when they stack up the plates for me. Like, I don't need you to play bad Tetris with the dinnerware."

"You should yell at them."

"I should," she agrees.

"I'm guilty of the bad Tetris, though. You can yell at me, too, if you want." I give her a playful smile.

She laughs. "Idiot."

We're naked in bed, lying side by side, talking. My fingers idly brush up and down her arm.

"I had a couple celebrating their 48th wedding anniversary. Just wanted to grab dinner and drinks."

"Wow. That's impressive." Her eyebrows lift. "Imagine tolerating somebody for that long."

"Yeah, imagine," I chuckle, grabbing her waist and pulling her closer to me. "My parents divorced when I was young. What about yours? Are they still together?"

"Not only are they still together and miserable, but she makes my father lunch every single day. Like the man can't be bothered to get up and make a damn sandwich."

"I can make my own lunch."

"Congratulations. I wasn't offering to make you a sandwich," she says.

"I can make you lunch, too."

She pins me with a stare, and I can't help but smile.

"I'm sorry," I say, because the truth is I'm engrossed in all these things she's sharing about herself.

"She is set on keeping a happy home. On not ruffling feathers. I'm a feather-ruffler by nature, so..." she trails off, shrugging as she does.

"I like it when you ruffle my feathers."

"You like it when I yell at you."

"Maybe." I laugh.

"You're just a glutton for punishment." She grabs the back of my neck, her fingers pressing into my pulse point, shifting the direction of the conversation. Too much at once.

"No." I quickly realize. "I think I'm just a glutton for something real." My eyes find hers and flare with too much promise and possibility. I'm sure she feels my pulse fluttering underneath her fingertips. If I were to feel hers, would it feel just as erratic? Would it be just as wild of a beat?

I lean in to kiss her slowly, and there's a flicker of a reminder that she's delicate, too. My hands hold her softly.

"You can be rough," she says. "You know I can handle it."

"No." I shake my head. "I want to be gentle with you."

And with that, every other emotion breaks through the surface.

I pin her wrists down with my hands, kissing them as I do. My fingers entwine with hers, knuckles turning white. She wraps herself around me like a vine, like the tattoo inked on my skin, keeping me together, giving me color.

I release my hand and move it down her body, fingertips gliding along lush skin. Goosebumps follow in their wake, and I love knowing the effect I have on her.

"God, look at how beautiful you are." The words come out in a rush, a breath of words that I can't seem to catch. "I like you like this."

"Yeah, I bet you do." She smirks.

When I slide into her, it's slow and delicious. I'm savoring every moment, watching her savor every inch. I move in and out of her at a glacial pace, sinking deeper each time. I groan softly, moving slowly, intentionally.

I let go of her wrists, and she pulls me down for a frantic kiss. She wants everything sped up and hurried, but I grab her wrists again, slowing everything down once more. I need this to last.

And *this* is beyond the sex, but I shouldn't even be thinking it.

Her hands trace the lines on my tattoo from my collarbone to my bicep. Her fingers dance on my skin as she follows the shape along my body.

My arms tremble with how hard I'm holding on, hovered over her, fucking her at an unhurried pace. I watch how I disappear into her, and I wonder what my life was like before I met her. Lifeless and dull.

She's spread out underneath me. Her hair is spilled sunshine on the pillow, her eyes darken, her mouth calls my name.

"I need words," she says in a rush.

"What words?"

"I need you to say stupid shit. Say something so I can yell at you."

But what she's saying is the silence is too much to handle. She wants the bickering and the banter, and I'd be lying if I said I didn't like it.

"Not this time." I shake my head.

A soft moan escapes her mouth. "Pain in the ass."

We're sleeping together for the fun of it, but my heart still desperately begs for her attention, for her to talk to me, for her to *like* me.

Suddenly her arm reaches over and roughly pulls open the drawer to her nightstand.

"The blue one is my favorite," she says.

She's letting me in, in more ways than one, and I jump at the opportunity.

"Yeah?" My voice is rough, eager, and excited.

I reach for the vibrator and turn it on, the buzz coming to life. I sit back on my heels and move the toy between us, settling it between her legs.

"How's that?" I ask, but I already see how it's affecting her. Body soft and wanting, flushed, sinking into the mattress. Hell, it's fucking affecting me. I don't know how much longer I'll last when she's squirming beneath me, whimpering my name. *Fuck.*

Suddenly, I feel her body tighten below me, and her back arches against the bed. Watching her fall apart never gets old, and when my own orgasm follows, I realize how incredibly intimate all of it feels. The very thing I'm sure she's trying to escape.

In a sea of sleeping together for the fun of it, I'm falling deeper and deeper into her life.

After I bring her a glass of water, and she takes a sip, she lies across the bed, parallel to me.

I didn't notice it at first, in the darkness of the room, but then I caught a glimpse of it one night—a tattoo spanning her right side along her ribcage. A thin line in cursive. I look closer. *Life is the big romance*, it reads.

"What's that?" I ask, my fingers reaching out to trace the words.

She startles a little, like nobody touches her like this. Novel movements with my hands. "What does it look like?"

"Give me more than that. What does it mean?"

I can see her debate how much she wants to tell me, but then she gives in. "It's from a short story I read when I was younger."

"Hell of a short story if you tattooed it on your skin," I say. "'Life is the big romance,'" I read. "As opposed to a romance with anyone else?" I give her a playful smile.

I move my fingers up and down her ribcage, following the delicate lines, and she lies perfectly still, watching me as I explore it.

"Does anybody else touch you like this?" I ask her, but my heart is in my throat.

Does anybody have access to her like this? Does anybody trace the lines of her tattoo, her ribs, her spine? Does anybody else get to hold her with firm hands, gripping like they could never let go?

I don't know why I ask her. I don't know if I can handle the answer. But maybe I want to hear it. I want to hear that others get this access, too. I want to hear that I'm nobody special, that I should remember the lines, the boundaries. This is, after all, nothing. This is, after all, meaningless sex.

But she doesn't tell me that.

She very slowly shakes her head no, and I sink deeper into it, let the quicksand slowly absorb me, as I lean over to kiss her, quietly and softly in the darkness. The darkness that's making this much easier for the both of us, I imagine.

But I don't imagine when she does speak, when she whispers against my shoulder, "Stay."

This is still exciting and electrifying. It's still fun.

But it's starting to burrow into me—how I could never tire of this. Together in her bed, together in her house. The thought of her is overwhelming, the reality of us together feels too good.

I'm not getting her out of my system, and a handful of times still won't be enough.

Nothing is normal now.

No, these feelings are worse than I thought. I think I'm falling for her, and I don't know what the hell to do about it.

Twenty-Four
AGOSTINA

WHEN I WAKE UP, I'm alone in my bed. A normal occurrence— I don't exactly make it a habit of waking up next to people. But I hear small noises coming from my kitchen and the faint smell of coffee brewing.

Gavin spent the night.

Maybe I was in a sex stupor, or in a trance as I watched him trace some years-old tattoo. As I got lost in his gentleness, in his soft body and my comfortable bed.

The one where the sheets ended up in a bundle on the floor again.

I roll out of bed and head to my kitchen, where I find him making me a cup of coffee. But how would he even know the proper ratio? He passes me the mug with a smile.

"I can make it myself." I frown.

"Such a ray of sunshine in the morning," he says as he walks over to me and kisses my forehead. "I know you can. But I like doing these things for you. They make me happy, so just let me."

This might be too domestic for me. I don't know what to do with it. Take me back to last night when he bent me over the bed.

I take a sip of coffee, and it's just how I like it: unbearably sweet, delightfully milky. Goddammit, it's delicious.

He smiles over his own mug as he watches me. Barefoot in my kitchen again, leaning against the counter, toe-to-toe with me. An ache blooms in my chest, building with each passing moment. Every time I see him smile, every time he's near me.

What the hell am I supposed to do with these feelings?

The position suddenly appears between us—lead bartender and the fight for it. Heavy and loud, letting its presence be known. What kind of person would I be if I turned it down for him? What kind of person would I be if I gave it up?

"What are you thinking about?" he asks.

"Want to go take a shower?" I throw the conversation in a different direction, away from me, my favorite party trick.

His smile grows bigger. "Yeah."

He watches me dry off and get dressed afterward, casually leaning back on the bed, grin gracing his face. At this rate, we're never going to get anything else done. But I've got work in a bit, so I brush my hair and get ready.

"Can I watch you do it?" he asks.

"Do what?"

"Your braid," he answers. "I'm kind of fascinated by it."

"What?" The word comes out as a huff of laughter.

"How did you learn to do it?"

"YouTube videos," I say, mildly confused by his infatuation with my hairdo.

His smile lights up his eyes. "I love your hair."

"I'm not really blonde," I blurt out.

He laughs. "I don't care. I just love it."

But it sounds like *it* could be easily replaced with another word, and my heart is about to fall out of my ass.

I move to do my hair, keeping my shaky hands occupied, and he just silently watches, leaning against the doorframe of my bathroom. When I'm done, he leans down and kisses me for what feels like hours. I don't stop it or cut it short. God, it feels too good.

"I'll see you at work, okay?" he says, and with that, he leaves, taking my sanity with him.

***

"Hey, Trevor," I say as I walk in to work.

"Hey, what's up?" He gives me a quick glance then does a double-take. "What's going on with your face?"

"What?"

"What is that?"

"What?" I emphasize, touching my face, trying to figure out what the hell he's talking about.

"Are you...smiling?"

My face drops. "Go fuck yourself, Trevor."

Later, Kelli notices how Gavin and I are avoiding eye contact, not even snippets of insults. She gathers her drink order and sets it on her tray.

"Something going on with you two?" she asks, narrowing her eyes.

"No," I say quickly.

"What?" Gavin blurts out. "Of course not."

"Uh-huh." She walks away.

"She's not convinced," he mumbles under his breath.

"Of course, she's not convinced. You look guilty as hell, you dumbass."

Nine thirty rolls around, and I gather my things to leave. Gavin and Trevor will be closing tonight, and I'm going home to change so Delfi and I can head to the milonga.

Once I make it home and shower, I throw on a simple skirt and top, an outfit I haven't worn in a while, and then I head out to meet Delfi.

We walk inside the venue and find a small table closer to the back. The music is already going, and the dance floor is mostly full. It doesn't take me long to spot her, out on the floor with Logan, but once I do, I can't look away. It's incredible.

She is so carefree, so passionate in her dancing. She moves with such purpose, running circles around this floor in our beloved grandmother's shoes. Delfi reaches for my arm and squeezes, her own gasp in action.

When Julie gets off the dance floor, she finds us staring, barely hiding, and thoroughly impressed.

"Oh my God, you were hiding this from us?" Delfi asks, wide-eyed.

Her answering smile is beaming. This Julie isn't shy or guilty or standing against the wall, she's proud. She's living in the moment in the best possible way.

"And look at this fucking dress!" I say, motioning to her wine-red dress with one shoulder and a slit up the back.

As we're admiring it, Logan walks up to us and passes Julie a cup of water. "Thought you could use some."

Delfi is probably screaming on the inside, and neither of us can help the wide grins on our faces.

Julie tries to shoo us away, telling us to go dance.

"I could introduce you to some people?" Logan offers.

Of course, Delfi says yes—she didn't attend many milongas when we were younger, but she'll never say no to something new or fun.

"Oh no," I say. "I am going to park it right here and keep watching you. I am thoroughly entertained."

But I stumble across Javier, and when he notices all of us, his eyes light up.

We pull up chairs to a large table, gathering around, talking loudly. When the conversation topic inevitably becomes about my grandmother, everything becomes that much more magical. How much she would have wanted to see Julie do this, how proud she would have been. I can hardly stand it and I'm watching it with my own eyes.

"Everybody still loves her," Julie says to us, quietly. "Everybody still talks so highly of her."

She is the one we strive to emulate every day—craving pieces of her life for our own lives.

Turns out Logan did, in fact, know her. Manny will lose his shit.

Julie and Logan move back to the dance floor, and I sit down to watch. He leads as she turns and twists, practically a professional, and I've never seen her so overjoyed. She's always been successful in her career, but this is something else altogether. A community, a new endeavor.

"That man is so in love," Delfina says, satisfied, with a shake of her head. "All my girls are falling in love."

"*All* your girls?" I look around. "*Who* are you talking about?"

She just laughs as Javier leads her to the floor.

I catch Gavin walk in, and I'm surprised to see he's changed for this. A pair of dress pants, a loose button-down with the sleeves rolled up to the elbows, and his smile. When he spots me sitting at the table, the smile grows wider. That one, my body makes note, is *my* smile.

I wonder if a smile has ever been mine like that. If, at some other point in my life, I could have claimed something like that solely for me. Not that I wanted to. No, I don't want any of it. So why, then, am I so quick to grab this one? Quick to scoop it up before anyone else does.

Delfi suspiciously falls into my line of sight, winking as she does, and I scowl as she dances away.

She spends most of the night dancing with Javier, laughing at her missteps, learning as she goes. When she takes a break after a tanda, he extends his hand out to me.

"Fine," I oblige.

Our tanda is simple, but it serves as a reminder of where I come from, where my grandmother found her joy. It's no surprise Julie's thrived here.

I vaguely remember steps she once taught me, and I leisurely move with Javier across the floor. He's patient, and gracious, leading me to the end of the dance expertly.

When I walk off the floor and head to the table, Gavin's eyes follow me, a slow perusal that feels like flame.

"You look..." He swallows. "Nice." His voice is deep, but it almost sounds like a question, an unsure compliment.

"Don't hurt yourself, bar boy."

"Let me try that again." His eyes move from top to bottom. "You look stunning."

"Better."

His mouth lifts on one side. "Exquisite."

"Fine."

He narrows his eyes. "Ravishing," he says with comical exaggeration.

"Stop talking."

His laughter is easy, a common thing between us, as he gestures for me to sit down. But there isn't a seat open nearby, instead filled with milonga regulars talking and catching up.

"Should I sit on your lap, then, bar boy?" I tease.

He shrugs. "I'd rather you sit on my face."

My own burst of laughter has become commonplace, too. "Even better."

The night ends around two in the morning, and I thank God I had the foresight to get my shift covered for tomorrow. Delfi carries her shoes to the car, Logan and Julie walk side by side, and I share a look with Gavin when we all say our goodbyes. Our own secret language now, one that says, *I'll see you later.*

His rhythmic knock on my door is one I know by heart. When I answer, he looks beyond happy to see me.

"Hey, Agostina."

I wasted years wishing I could be a Jessica or a Jennifer only to realize my name was beautiful all along. And it has never sounded more beautiful, more perfect than it does now. Goosebumps erupt along my arms and he notices them, of course, he does. His bright smile shines for me, and it's like he's telling me everything I need to know with just one look.

I reach for his hand and pull him in, bringing his mouth to mine immediately.

And later, when my knees settle on either side of his face, I fall into nothing but absolute, shattering bliss as he feasts on me.

Twenty-Five
AGOSTINA

I LOAD MY PLATE up with empanadas and take a big bite of one as I sit in my chair.

Tía Maria sits at the head of the table, pushing everybody to fill their plates.

"You know who called me?" she asks, setting her elbows on the table, getting comfortable. "Javier."

I instantly look to Julie, eyes wide and concerned. Not Javier and his fucking big mouth.

"He was so proud of you, Julieta," she says. "And he said I must be so proud of you, too, taking after abuela and following in her steps."

I catch Cecilia's surprised smile, but Julie is pale as a ghost, silently shutting down.

"So, I had to tell him that unfortunately my daughter hadn't told me anything. Guess I didn't deserve to know what was going on."

She's looking for a fight, something I know all too well, and I'm not one to back down.

"She doesn't have to tell you what she's doing," I say with bite.

But Maria accuses Julie of lying, and Julie, finally, unexpectedly, fights back. Words are thrown out like daggers, an uncomfortable family dinner taking place. My father keeps his head down, eating his food, chronically indifferent. My tío Julio tries to keep Maria's anger at bay, sensible and level-headed, a foreign concept to me.

Because if there's anything I know how to do, it's throw more fuel into the fire.

"This is so stupid. Who fucking cares what she's doing? She's a grown adult. But since you're all so interested in how she's been deceiving you, at least take a look for yourselves."

I pull out my phone and search for a video I took of Julie at the milonga. I hold it out to show Maria, but her mouth stays firm.

"Look at your daughter," I urge. "Look at the joy. And the talent."

My mother stares at me in warning, but I don't care. Tensions rise, and more secrets come out—like the trip to San Diego—and Maria knocks Julie and her newfound joy down to the fucking ground.

Julie leaves shortly after, quiet and defeated, and I'm left pissed off.

"That was so unnecessary. Es tu hija, Maria," I say to her.

My mom tries to shush me, but I can see the pain in Cecilia's eyes, too. The shock around the room at everything we just witnessed. Nobody knew what Julie was doing, and I understand why she wanted to keep the secret.

And then my mother wordlessly picks up my father's plate and starts clearing the rest of the table. Never ruffling feathers, never speaking up. A life of servitude. Tía Maria follows, and I get up and storm out.

Fuck this.

I pick up my phone and make a call before I'm even out of the driveway, and it rings only once before the person on the other line picks up.

"Hey, Agos," Leo says when he answers, and I'm instantly so annoyed that he's far away. That he chose to move to another county.

"You're an asshole," I say.

"What the hell?"

"You missed Sunday dinner again." He very rarely makes it out to family dinner unless it's a holiday.

"I know, I'm sorry."

"And Julie is dancing," I throw out, because I'm so frustrated and I need to get all of it off my chest.

"Julie's dancing?"

"She's dancing at the fucking milonga with a tango instructor that she met and is definitely involved with."

"Oh shit," he says, surprise in his voice. "That's amazing."

"It would be, except for the fact that she was keeping it a secret and Javier blew her cover and now Maria's pissed and Julie's defeated."

"Good God, I'm missing a lot."

"You are, Leo. You really are and that's the point and I'm so mad at you for it and I know that you wanted to move away and I get it, I really do, but it fucking sucks." My voice almost cracks.

"Are you saying you miss me?"

"I'm saying you suck. That's why I called."

His sigh on the other line is loud. "I miss you, too, Agos. I'll be there next Sunday."

And with that, I hang up.

But with my phone still in hand, I reach for comfort and familiarity, the habit for calming myself. I pull up Gavin's number and send one simple, concise text.

Come over.

So he does, after his shift, walking into my apartment like this is his favorite place to be. The cause of my incandescent rage has become the one to soothe it.

"Thought you couldn't stand me," he says with a lift of his lips.

"I thought I couldn't either."

He kisses me, and I force myself not to think about how at peace I instantly feel.

Twenty-Six
AGOSTINA

"It was awful. She looked so heartbroken, I couldn't handle it." I reach for a rock and lift my body, grunting as I do.

Manny follows next to me. "I can't handle that you dragged me here."

We decided to use the rock climbing coupons, much to his chagrin. But I needed to get out of my house, and I was too angry to do something calming.

"You should have seen her, Manny. She *was* my grandmother out on that floor. It was amazing."

"There's no guilt like Hispanic mom guilt," he says, shaking his head.

"God, just unbelievably talented. And my aunt was a self-righteous asshole."

He grunts as he lifts his body to the next rock, getting higher on the wall.

"My mom, too. Everybody sucked." I huff, a little out of breath, as I move up the wall.

"Maybe we shouldn't talk and rock climb," he suggests.

"A tragedy."

"How's Gavin doing?"

"Why are you asking me?" I ask, sounding too defensive.

"Because you work the bar with him," he answers, as if it's obvious. Then, a little quieter, he says, "Also, because you're probably still fucking him."

The accusation catches me by surprise, so much so that when I reach for the next rock, I slip and fall, yelping as I go down. I land wrong, and a pain shoots up my foot, letting me know that yeah, I'm fucked.

"Shit!" I scream out, and Manny belays down practically in despair as I writhe in pain on the floor.

"No, no, no," Manny repeats over and over as a staff member runs over to us. A crowd is forming. This is great.

"I swear to God, Alexis was right," he says in a panic. "That coupon was cursed from the beginning."

"I'm fine." I wave it away as I try to get up. But the staff members keep me down, worried I've severely broken something.

"I'll take her to the urgent care down the street now," Manny lets them know, and I groan in annoyance as he gets me up and takes me to his car.

"This is so stupid," I grumble in the passenger seat.

"Cursed. Coupon," he emphasizes. "Do you want me to call anybody?"

"No." I shake my head. "Why don't you just take me home?"

"And then find out you have a broken foot, and you can never work again? I would never."

"Okay, maybe a little dramatic."

"I already feel at fault for throwing that Gavin question at you."

"You're right. This is your fault," I say as I wince in pain.

"Turns out I can talk too much," Manny says, practically distressed.

I huff out a laugh before dealing with my own worries. "Manny, I don't have good enough insurance for this, and you know that. God, is this the moment that I start to feel like a loser?" I talk so much shit. Maybe I need a 401k.

"Let's see what they say." He turns into the parking space and walks me in.

It's not too full, so I check in and grab the clipboard then find a seat in a corner.

"Never thought I'd say this, but thank God Steve's been putting me on those large parties," I mumble as I'm filling out the paperwork, resigned to paying a large copay.

An older man has a severe coughing fit, while a kid sneezes and sniffles. Manny reaches in my bag for some hand sanitizer.

"By the way, you were right." I lean closer to him. "I am still fucking Gavin."

"Fucking hell," he mutters, shaking his head. "I mean, I'm not surprised. But also, I am."

"Yeah, well, it's just sex, and you're sworn to secrecy."

"Just sex? Really?" He gives me a disbelieving look.

"Yes, really," I emphasize, just as the nurse calls me to the back.

After what feels like an eternity of being here, the doctor concludes, "Just a sprain."

"Great, thanks," I say, moving quickly to get out of here and go home.

"But"—she stops me—"I would recommend bandaging it

up and staying off of it for at least a week."

"Sure, sounds good." I nod, knowing damn well I'm not going to do that.

"Don't even try getting out of it," Manny mumbles in my ear.

"He's right. You could risk making it worse, and then you'll really be on bed rest."

Bed rest sounds like the worst possible fucking thing ever.

"Right, well, I also have to work." And how am I going to manage that if I need to be off my foot?

"See if you can do minimal movements at the bar," Manny says. "Make sure Steve doesn't put you on any parties."

"I'll have the nurse discharge you." She leaves the room, and I sit back and throw my arm over my eyes.

"You know, we won't all be there forever," Manny says, breaking the silence.

I open my eyes. "The Ivy, you mean?"

"Yeah."

"I know," I sigh. He doesn't come out and say it, but what he means is what's the point in holding on so fiercely to my convictions? What's the point in fighting for something that won't matter if or when I choose to leave? It's another tía Cecilia speech. "That place has been a big part of my life."

"For all of us. But we don't need that place to hold us together. Our relationships will thrive long after."

I close my eyes again.

"I've just been thinking about your frustrations, about how so much of it has been due to Steve. I don't think he's going anywhere, and maybe I was wrong to want to keep you there for my own personal benefit."

"Are you saying I make your life at The Ivy complete? Are you saying you can't function without me?" I push.

"Yeah, that's exactly what I'm saying," he says dryly, and I laugh.

"You're not keeping me there, I'm keeping myself there. And maybe some of that—or a lot of that, I guess—has to do with all of you."

"Are we talking about feelings?" he says, almost aghast. "Disgusting."

He chuckles then says softly, "I might be cutting back."

I open my eyes once more, sitting up to look at him.

"I'm finishing up my certifications, and I've talked to a couple of schools."

Manny has been interested in teaching since I met him. Serving was always supplemental.

"That's great, Manny." I give him a smile, but there's sadness just beneath it. He's making his way out before me.

Is it finally time for all of us to grow up and move on?

The nurse comes in with discharge papers, and it goes quicker than I expected. Manny helps me out of the building, guiding me as I hobble to the car.

"I'm not staying out of work for a week," I tell him, my voice cracking slightly. I clear it, but it feels raw. Sore and uncomfortable as I swallow.

"I'd like it if you took care of yourself, rubia."

"I always do," I sigh, annoyed. "I'm so tired. I think I need a nap. That rock climbing took it out of me."

He parks in the visitor spot and helps me out of the car.

Manny wraps his arm around my waist and guides me as I limp to my apartment. I fumble around for my keys and let us both in.

I hobble to the kitchen for a glass of water, taking a deep breath as I lean against the counter. "Sorry about this," I say, motioning to my foot.

"You're okay," he says. "Let's order some pizza and hang out on the couch. I'll text Alexis."

"Yeah, all right." But I feel less than enthusiastic, an unusual, unfamiliar feeling where I'd rather just sleep.

"Not all right," he says, looking at me.

"I'm just tired." I sneeze. "And these allergies are annoying me right now."

"I think I'll just leave you to it, then," he says softly. "But are you sure you'll be okay?"

"I'll call you if anything. Delfi's not too far, either."

"You could call Gavin," he suggests, and I glare at him.

That's not what our relationship is, I reason, and I'm not going to bother him with this.

He grabs my soft blanket and sets it on the couch along with a mountain of snacks from my cabinets. "That way you don't have to get up."

I chuckle softly as he leaves everything in order for me. "Stop feeling guilty, Manny. I'm fine." I give him a hug. "Thanks."

When he closes the door behind him, I fall into my couch, and in no time, I'm fast asleep.

Twenty-Seven
GAVIN

MANNY RUNS HIS PALM along his forehead as he says, "She sprained her ankle. It could have been so much worse."

We're gathered around the bar as dinner shifts are set to begin.

"Cursed coupon," Alexis emphasizes.

"That's what I said!"

"Is she all right?" I interject, worried.

"She's okay. She just needs to rest and stay off her foot for a couple of days, so you can imagine how that's going to be."

I'm upset she didn't reach out to me about it, but I know I don't have any right to be.

"Oh shit, she's going to be miserable," Alexis says.

"So miserable," Manny agrees. "She was going to push through it and come into work anyway."

"But?" Trevor leans in.

"She woke up with a fever," he winces, and everybody collectively groans.

"Shit," Trevor says.

"So, she called out sick, too," Manny adds, which only leads to gasps from everybody in the group.

"I take it she never calls out sick?" I ask.

Everybody shakes their head no.

"Alright, let's get through tonight, then," Trevor says with a sigh. "Gavin, you ready?"

I nod, but I think about her running circles around this restaurant and spending weekends out in the city with friends. I think about how she surrounds herself with people whenever she can. Laughs loudly, dances any chance she gets, makes plans with everybody. And I worry some more as I make my own plan to go see her after work.

"Let's order some food from next door and bring it to her," Alexis suggests.

"Good idea. Maybe some soup? They have clam chowder," Manny adds.

But they grimace in response, and so I humbly throw in my own suggestion. "I can go over and bring her some soup. I don't mind."

"Aw, Gavin. That's sweet," Alexis says. "That would be perfect."

"Alright." I nod and get to work on restocking garnishes.

"Don't you need her address?"

"Oh." I still. "Right. You can give me her address."

But Manny slaps the bar top and whispers, "Christ, you are a terrible liar."

"Really terrible," Alexis agrees.

My jaw drops as I look between them both. "She told you, didn't she?"

"To be fair, I guessed," he says then leans in. "It may or may not be why she fell."

"Oh God." I run my hand down my face. "Okay, well,

Trevor doesn't know," I say, hopeful to at least keep my end of the bargain.

"Oh, I definitely know," Trevor admits as he sets a cocktail down for service. "I'm not going to tell her that I know. But I know."

I throw my hands up in defeat. "Are we that obvious?"

"Yes," all three of them answer in unison.

"This is the restaurant business. Everybody knows the color of your underwear before you put it on," Manny says with a shrug.

With that, Alexis and Manny grab the drinks for their tables and move to drop them off, and Trevor comes to stand next to me.

"You sure you know what you're doing?" he asks me quietly.

"Not even a little bit."

He nods. "Just don't want to see either of you get hurt, that's all."

"Who's hurting who?" I ask.

But he doesn't answer as he walks away to greet a guest.

***

"Hey, Gavin. Can I talk to you?" Steve asks me as I'm wrapping everything up for the night.

"Sure."

"My office," he says, and I follow him to the back. "Listen. I think I'm going to be firing some servers," he says quietly. "T is my best server, so—"

"I'll take it." I don't know what comes over me, but I don't even let him finish the sentence.

"You'll take what?"

"The server spot. I'll take it. I know you want to give it to her, but she deserves better than that and you know it."

He sits back with a knowing smirk, and it pisses me off.

"Were you ever going to give her that position?" I ask.

"Of course, I was," he says dismissively. "But I have to admit, it's been nice to see her step her game up a little bit. Knowing you were in the running for it."

"With all due respect, Steve, it seems like she's been great at that job since before I started here."

"Something going on with you two?" He narrows his eyes. "You can tell me."

I just give him an exasperated sigh in response. We're not really friends anymore, no matter if he wants us to be. He's my boss, and he sucks. And it's frustrating that it took me so long to right the wrong.

"I'd be careful if I were you," he says when I don't answer.

"What does that mean?"

"You don't know her like I do. She's got a bit of a history, you know what I mean?"

"You really are an asshole, Steve," I blurt out. "Give me the server spot. Or don't. But she gets lead bartender." And with that, I get up and walk out.

Twenty-Eight
GAVIN

THERE'S A GROCERY STORE open late by the restaurant, so I manage to grab a bag of things before I head over to her place.

As I knock on the door, I look down at my bags of groceries and am hit with a sudden realization that I don't know what her kitchen is equipped with. I've stumbled around it half-heartedly, filling a glass with water, but now I'm kicking myself for not paying more attention.

Just then, the door opens to a shocked T.

"Hi." I give her my friendliest smile.

"I'm not having sex with you." Her voice is raspy; her nose is red and stuffed.

My smile falls and gives way to confusion. "That's not why I'm here."

"Then why are you here?" Now she's perplexed.

"That's the only reason I would be here?" My eyebrows shoot up.

"Yeah." She sneezes loudly, sniffling in the aftermath.

"You look terrible."

"I'm sorry, did you come to insult me?"

"I brought soup." I hold up bags of groceries, moving to change the subject. "Well, ingredients to make soup."

Her brows knit together. "What?"

"I just told you—"

"How did you know I was sick?" She crosses her arms.

"Manny. He was telling everybody about your foot, too." I look down and notice it bandaged up. She's on one foot, not putting much pressure on the other.

She rolls her eyes. "That asshole."

"Why didn't you tell me about this?" I ask, unable to hide the hurt in my voice.

"Gavin," she huffs, exasperated.

I'm concerned about her putting more stress on her foot, so I push it to the side as I've done with everything else. "You shouldn't be on your feet. Can I come in?"

She stands there for a moment before she gives up and says, "Fine."

Maybe she's in too much of a flu fog to fight anymore, but once I step in and close the door behind me, I find her not resting but rearranging her furniture instead.

"What the hell are you doing?" Now I'm even more stressed.

"Moving furniture."

"You have the flu and a sprained ankle. Sit down."

"You don't tell me what to do." She moves her hands to her hips.

"Jesus Christ, not this again. Sit down."

"No."

"You are stubborn as fuck, you know that?"

She shrugs then pushes her couch from one end of the wall to the other, resulting in a big coughing fit.

My blood pressure is rising as I stand here. "I can't handle this. Please come sit down." I motion to the couch she's trying to maneuver.

"This wasn't part of the agreement, Gavin."

"What agreement?"

"This." She waves a hand between us. "I don't need a fuck buddy turned caretaker."

The words shouldn't sting, but they do. I don't know what I expected, considering she didn't even tell me about what happened. I had to hear it from Manny.

"But I'm your friend, too, aren't I?" I say, fighting for a part in her life. "And friends help each other."

She sighs in what sounds like defeat.

"You don't even have the energy to properly fight with me. Let me just make you some soup."

She plops down on the couch loudly and wraps herself up in a comically large blanket that looks like the softest thing I've ever seen. There are pink and purple flowers all over it. A box of tissues sits nearby, with several crumpled ones littering the coffee table. I gingerly pick them up to toss them in the trash.

I make my way to the kitchen and start to unpack my grocery bags. I shuffle around, opening drawers and cabinets, looking for what I need. Her kitchen is surprisingly well-stocked.

"Do you cook?" I ask her.

"Sometimes," she answers, but doesn't elaborate.

She turns on the TV, and I gather a cutting board and a knife to chop up some vegetables.

"When my brother was younger, I would make him this soup, too." I stir the onions in the pot, the fragrant smell filling the apartment, and I think about those years when I took care of him relentlessly. When the divorce didn't do anybody any favors, I took it upon myself to make sure he was okay.

And then I got sucked into my previous job and left him alone.

"How is Logan doing?" she asks.

"He's doing really well. It makes me happy to see it." That's the truth, too. I've seen the light come back to his eyes; I've seen his passion emerge again. "He's doing those private lessons with Julie."

"Is that what the kids call it these days?"

I laugh as I put my hands up. "I'm not going to intercept in his sex life."

"She's happy, too. Happier than I've ever seen her," she says.

"Yeah. They deserve it."

"She's finally doing something for herself. My aunt was kind of an asshole about it, though."

"Oh?"

"Javier has a big mouth," she explains. "My aunt didn't know what was going on, and Julie didn't tell her, for good reason. My aunt can be an asshole. Do you know she got so mad at me once for eating empanada filling out of the pot?"

I shake my head no.

"She wouldn't shut up about it for like six months. Anyway, I'm happy for them." She grabs a tissue and sneezes into it, sniffling in the aftermath.

"Did you take anything? Do you need me to go get you medicine?"

She looks over at me, inexplicably confused, and answers, "No. I've got stuff here."

She snuggles into her blanket, watching TV, and I love how comfortable she's become with me. How she's sharing stories of her family. Maybe it's the cold medicine.

"Soup's almost ready," I call out.

"Great," she says, not looking away from the TV.

I ladle the soup into bowls and bring them over to her on the couch. I set them on the coffee table and go back to the kitchen for spoons.

"What is it?" she asks.

"Just chicken and vegetable soup."

She sits up and leans closer to the table. I watch her scoop a spoonful of soup and blow to make it cooler. When she slurps and swallows, her eyes widen slightly in surprise. She nods and goes back for a second spoonful, the warmth in my chest growing bigger.

"This isn't terrible, Gavin."

"The highest honor," I say with a smile.

"Are you buttering me to tell me you're getting lead bartender?" she asks.

My hand stills. "We're not going to talk about that right now," I tell her.

She furrows her brow. "Why not?"

"Because it's not important. It's not why I'm here, and I don't care."

She looks at me curiously as she slurps another spoonful of soup. "You've got it now, I'm sure. I sprained my ankle. I lost the game."

"Wasn't a game," I mutter under my breath.

I know she wants to say something in response, but I get

ahead of it.

"Should we put on some *Columbo*?" I offer, and I don't miss the small smile she tries to hide under her blanket.

Once this is over, we'll have to talk about the position—the one that Steve threw on my lap, the one that led us to this situation, the one that brought me right to her. But I've made my decision, and I'll go to sleep knowing it was the right one.

When we're done eating, I clear the table and start loading the dishwasher to help.

"What the hell are you doing?" she asks, watching me from the couch.

"Loading the dishwasher." I point to the dirty dishes.

"No, I see that. But why are you doing it like that?"

"Like what?"

"Who taught you how to load a dishwasher?"

"Nobody," I answer.

"Yeah, clearly."

I put the dish down. "Are you going to complain about me cleaning up or...?"

"Can I show you how to do it?"

"No," I argue. "You need to rest."

"You are not going to boss me around in my own house. I will kick you out."

I set the dish on the counter. "Fine."

I follow her instructions, loading the dishes in proper order and cleaning her kitchen until it's sparkling.

Back on the couch, she turns to me. "You don't have to stay, Gavin. It's okay. I can call Delfi."

"You know how you love your friends? How you rely on

them? I can be that for you, too. I'm here, T."

I see her working up an argument, opening her mouth to say something, but then she stops herself.

"You don't have to be so strong all the time, you know. Tell me what more I can do. You've never been shy about bossing me around."

That gets a small smile out of her.

"Sorry I didn't tell you about this," she says.

"I know you don't owe it to me, but I want to be here for you. Whenever you need me."

She studies me for a moment, with a red nose and tired eyes, but I have nothing to hide.

"Fine," she decides, expelling a breath.

"Good."

"And your soup was delicious." She says it quietly, like she's ashamed to even admit it.

This gets a laugh out of me. "I'm glad you liked it. I'll make you soup whenever you want."

She continues silently watching whatever is on TV, but soon enough, she sniffles next to me, and I immediately reach over for a tissue. When I hand it to her, I realize she's not sniffling because she's sick. She's sniffling because she's crying.

She wipes her eyes quickly, but I already caught her.

"Hey," I say softly, moving closer to her on the couch.

"Don't."

I sit back to give her space. "Are you hurt?"

"I hate this," she grumbles through tears.

"Being sick? Of course, you do. Nobody likes being sick."

"No. Being stuck," she says louder. "Feeling like I can't go anywhere or do anything. I'm stuck in this house with this cold and my foot, and I don't want to be here. I want to be out. I want to be doing something. Being productive."

And that's it. That's the root of it. A vulnerable admission in the midst of unfortunate events.

"Do you ever get tired of it?" I ask. "Do you ever want to just be alone?"

"No."

But I wonder if what she likes is keeping her life busy to avoid feeling.

"I spent many years alone—traveling, working, selling. So, I understand the need for noise, but I also value the quiet."

"Is that from the latest self-help book you're reading?"

"You have a hard time with silence, don't you?" I ask.

"I love talking to people," she argues. "I love being with my friends. Hanging out with them everywhere," she says.

I nod. "Yeah, I know. But right now, your body is demanding rest, so let me help you with that. I know all about sitting on a couch and mindlessly watching TV for days on end."

"So, you're saying I've fallen to your level?"

"Exactly. Lucky for you, I can offer guidance." I reach for the remote and pull up Netflix, scrolling for a documentary I think she'll like. "Want to learn about the California redwoods?"

"God, how do you do this?"

"Without this much complaining."

She blows a raspberry, and it makes me laugh.

"Oh, T," I sigh, and it makes her frown. Lips turned down at the corners, eyes soft. "Let me tell you what I know. I love how you live your life. I want to emulate it. I want to be a part of it," I say, an admission. "But it doesn't mean that life is always meant to be lived fast-paced or sped up. There's beauty in the present. There's comfort at home." I shrug.

She sits in silence for a moment, balking at me, then says, "Delfi is rubbing off on you."

I sigh. Maybe I thought she would care about what I have to say right now, but I shouldn't push anything. She's sick, she's feverish. She's not doing great.

"Being vulnerable is so gross." She scowls.

I smile. "I like it."

"Of course, you do," she says with an eye roll, then thinks about it before deciding slowly, "I want to learn about the California redwoods."

And with that surprise, I select the documentary and it begins.

When the documentary is done, I look over and she's asleep. Bundled up in her blanket, stretched out on the couch.

I'm so goddamn enamored with her.

As she sleeps, I get off the couch and clean up around her apartment, careful not to mess with any important things. I walk over to the wall of pictures again, one of my favorite places in this apartment.

I look at the pictures, the snapshots in time. I look at her vibrant life, fast-paced and frenzied energy. Of course, she hates being stuck here. She'd rather be out there living.

I turn to keep moving, but my eyes snag on a picture. I almost missed it. Tucked in between all the other ones is the picture I took of us on the Ferris wheel. There I am, in her life, important enough to be on her wall.

And I selfishly wonder, what would it take to make it into her heart?

There's a leather-bound journal resting on one of her shelves. It looks out of place, like she may have been looking through it and didn't put it back. It's out in the open, over-stuffed, and I see postcards peeking out of it.

I glance over my shoulder and find T still sleeping, so I pick it up and take a peek. It's a travel journal, and as I turn each page, I find a city with notes and pictures attached. There are additional notes added in her handwriting, but the pages have original script. This isn't hers, but it looks like she's been following it precisely.

I keep flipping the pages, immersed in this story that I know nothing about. But I want to know about it, I want to know about her.

"What are you doing?"

I jump at the sound of her voice, and I'm clearly guilty as hell as I hold this journal in my hands. Her voice isn't angry, though. And a part of me wonders if she left it out for somebody to find. If she'd rather somebody look through it without having to speak about it out loud.

"Sorry," I say, half-heartedly.

"You don't sound it," she says with a smirk. "What time is it?"

"It's close to one in the morning." Time flew by as the documentary played on, as she fell asleep and I cleaned up.

"You need sleep," she says. More deflection.

"I'm fine," I say. "You should go to bed."

"No, *I'm* fine."

"Baby," I say gently, a slip up. Something I've only allowed myself to call her during sex, but here I've said it out in the open, in conversation. And her eyelids flutter at the sound of it. "Your body needs rest."

I set the journal down, and her eyes follow the motion. There are so many questions, as there always are when it comes to her, and this time, missing answers. But I let it go for now as I walk over, help her stand and guide her to her room. I move the sheets over and motion for her to lie down.

She does, snuggling under the covers, deeply sighing as her body hits the mattress. I tuck her in, arranging the sheets so she's as comfortable as can be, savoring this moment where she's letting me care for her. She stares up at me like she's seeing me for the first time, like I'm magic and she can't believe I'm here.

My heart nearly stops.

"I'll take the couch. Is that okay?" I whisper.

"That's okay," she mumbles, eyelids too heavy to remain open.

And with that, she's deep asleep again.

Twenty-Nine
AGOSTINA

By the morning, I feel like I've finally cleared through the fog. The fever is gone, and the pain in my ankle has mostly subsided.

I gently limp out of my bedroom to find Gavin in my kitchen in his boxers, making me coffee again.

Fucking hell.

Suddenly, I need him here. Everywhere. In this apartment, in my life.

"How are you feeling?" he asks.

Disastrous. "Better."

"Want to eat breakfast?"

"I'm not sure." My stomach is in knots.

Maybe I still have a fever. Maybe I'm sick and confused.

"I can make you some toast?" he offers.

"Okay." I give in.

I hobble over to the couch, and Gavin passes me a mug of perfectly brewed coffee just how I like it. The toast is delightfully buttered, and the rest of me is trying not to panic as I enjoy the best breakfast I've had in what feels like forever. I'm worried I'll get too used to this.

I spot the journal on the table and remember last night through the feverish fog. He found it and was reading it as I woke up startled on the couch.

He sips his own coffee and eyes me over the mug. The silence between us is never too much. It feels like worn-in shoes, my favorite sweater, something I could live in forever.

"I got my grandmother's travel journal when she passed away," I start.

"Tango dancing grandmother?"

I nod. "The very one. Did you meet her too?" I ask and hold my breath for the answer. I don't know how I'd take it if I found out he'd met her, too.

"No." He shakes his head. "That was Logan's department, not mine. I knew of her, with her mentorship and all, and Logan spoke so highly of her. He really loved her."

I hastily take a sip of my coffee, an attempt to push everything down.

He picks up the journal and brings it closer, opening it up to flip through its soft pages.

"So, I decided I wanted to visit these places, too. I wanted to follow in her steps, or something. I don't know." It sounds dumb when I say it out loud, like I couldn't be bothered to plan my own travels. Or like I couldn't let her be.

"That sounds like a lot of adventures," he says with a smile. And I should know by now that he's not going to make me feel dumb about anything. "So, you do all of this alone?" he asks.

"Sometimes Delfi comes. Manny joined me once. But otherwise, yeah."

"Doesn't it get lonely?" Nobody has ever asked me that before. Nobody has ever assumed it, but he sees through me, and I think he always has.

"Not really," I tell him, but it does.

"Which has been your favorite place to visit?"

"From the journal?"

I got possession of this journal two years ago, but I've been traveling much longer than that. My wall of pictures documents years of sightseeing through the world.

"I loved Barcelona. I loved Seattle. I loved San Diego, too. Julie's going to love it there."

"Wow." He keeps flipping pages, slowly working his way through, perusing every story on every piece of paper, moving to the end.

"No," I blurt out, placing my palm on the open journal.

He lifts his hands up. "Sorry," he says, mildly concerned, somewhat confused.

"You can't see the last page," I tell him then clarify, "Nobody's seen the last page."

"And what's supposedly on this mysterious last page?"

I hesitate, not wanting to give up any more secrets. But he's here. He's been here. And even though it pains me to admit, there's nobody else I'd want here right now but him. "Her favorite place," I answer.

His eyebrows lift. "That's a big deal."

"I know." I move my hand from the journal, and he gingerly sets his back down.

"How close are you to the last page?" he asks.

"A couple of trips left. I kind of..." I hesitate to finish but keep going. "I've been prolonging it. I don't want it to end."

"Why not? What happens when it ends?"

What happens is that I won't know what to do. I'll have to

close the journal and really say goodbye to her.

"You could keep going, T. You could keep traveling the whole world," he says with enthusiasm. "I'd travel the world with you."

"Oh yeah?" I chuckle.

"I'd go anywhere with you."

"They all say that." It's dismissive, I know. An attempt to push away every deep feeling I've uncovered since waking up. Probably since before then, but I figure I was maybe a little bit blissfully aware back then.

"Don't do that. Don't lump me in with all the other boys you've dated."

He doesn't let me dismiss it—him or these growing uncomfortable feelings.

His messy hair is falling into his eyes, so I reach over and brush it back. He grabs my hand and kisses my palm softly.

The tension is a force between us, and I thought it came from our work. From the adrenaline of a busy night, the fight for the position. But here in the quiet of my house, cozy and warm, it still feels the same between us. The fire burns just as hot, maybe even hotter.

"You've been everywhere. It's amazing."

"Then why do I still feel so empty?" I whisper.

He tilts his head to look at me, my palm still along his jaw. "You've done so much."

"Then why doesn't it feel like enough?"

"What are you worried about?" he asks, furrowing his brows.

"That life will pass me by if I don't take hold of it," I painfully, embarrassingly admit. That I will look back and regret not doing more. That I will never feel productive enough. That I might never make her proud.

"Does anybody else know about this?" He motions to the journal, but *this* could be a number of things.

Because I realize there are things I hadn't even told Manny or Alexis or Trevor. There are things that I've confided in him and him alone.

I shake my head no.

His hands gently cradle my face, holding me like I'm some delicate thing. Like I'm worthy of softness.

I let out a shaky breath. "You don't get to tear down my walls, Gavin."

"Why not?" he whispers.

"Because," I say quietly, "you could destroy me."

"I wouldn't."

"You don't know that."

"Let me in," he pleads. "I want to take care of you."

"You can bend me over the couch again," I tease, but he doesn't let me.

"I want to really take care of you."

"With more soup?"

He smiles. "With more soup. Give you a soft place to land."

I ignore the lump in my throat. "I don't need anybody to take care of me," I say softly, but there's barely any fight in it.

"I know you don't. But…" He kisses me gently. "Maybe you could want me."

There he is, fighting for a way in, when all I ever do is fight for a way out.

"I don't think I'm soft enough for this."

He shakes his head firmly, somehow adamant about everything when it comes to me. "That's not true."

He grabs me by the waist and lifts me up onto the counter.

"Got to keep you off your feet," he says softly. "Doctor's orders."

I keep my legs apart, giving him space to stand between them. His hands graze the tops of my thighs, maneuvering under the hem of my oversize T-shirt, and he leans in to kiss me.

His palms move higher, his fingers falling into the space between my legs, down my center, tracing my wetness, making me shake.

"What are we doing?" I practically beg. I'm praying for an answer that will give me some kind of explanation. Some kind of clarity into what is happening.

"You tell me, T," he says, but his words are strained.

His fingers ease in and out of me slowly, a curling, punishing fire burning hotter with every touch. His lips are suctioned to my throat, breathing harshly. Breathing life into me.

"This doesn't feel like fun anymore," I say, swallowing thickly.

With his thick fingers deep inside me, my body is a tidal wave of aching, relentless emotion.

"What does it feel like?"

"I want the control," I say, admitting defeat.

He huffs out a disbelieving laugh. "Baby, you've got all the control."

"I feel turned upside down," I whisper, pleading. My orgasm is building; my walls are falling apart.

"And I don't? God, you don't realize how you own me." His fingers move almost impossibly deeper, and his lips hover over mine. "I can't think of anyone else but you. I don't want to be near anyone else but you. Every time I look at you, my heart swells. I think it might explode with how much I feel for you."

Our eyes meet in what feels like complete panic on my end, reckless free-falling. But he just kisses me roughly, his hand working in tandem with his tongue.

My kitchen counter is a fucking altar of bad decisions, and his fingers are bringing me to the edge of oblivion. This is about as close to a religious experience as I get.

"Please, come for me," he begs, voice strained, like he's so fucking tortured. "I need you to."

But what I hear, almost shamefully, is *I need you, too.*

And with that, I fall apart in his arms, his mouth on my neck, my legs open just for him. I feel the intense build and the almost violent crash. The flood of relief.

My orgasm is loud, an unwavering torture as he fucks me with his fingers, as he whispers *baby* against my skin over and over again. Like he's calling me to him. Like he owns that word and nobody will ever be able to call me that again.

Nobody but him.

And after I float down, there's the safety of his arms. The feeling of being home.

My arms wrap around him tightly, the most stability I've ever felt. If I didn't believe in anything before, I worry that I absolutely, undoubtedly, do now.

Once I come down, he slowly moves his fingers and shifts to pick me up and carry me right back to bed.

I'm boneless, satiated, in a fog of desire.

"You can stay again tonight. If you want," I say. The simplest of words, but it feels like I carved my heart out and set it on a platter for him.

And he knows it, too.

"Yeah." He kisses my forehead softly as he enters my bedroom. "I want." He places me on the bed, pulls my shirt over my head, and then lets me watch as he takes his boxers off. "I want so much, T, I can barely fucking handle it."

I want to wrap up that desire and hold it close to me forever. The most terrifying notion of all.

I grab his face instead and bring him down for a deep kiss. I like the solid weight of him, the feel of how I sink under his body.

"I don't like you," I tell him, like I've told him many times before. But this time, the meaning is just beneath it, woven between the familiar words. The fine line, the implication is clear.

"I don't like you, either," he whispers, smiling like it's a secret between the two of us, a revelation in a new light.

And when I rest my head on his arm, I'm surprised by how content I feel to be here, to be home.

We spend the rest of the day wrapped in each other, making a mess of my bed, and an even bigger mess of my heart.

Thirty
AGOSTINA

Every morning, the coffee tastes better than the last. I wish I could hate it, but my heart is melting. I wish I could push him away when it gets too uncomfortable, but I don't want him to leave. He doesn't upset my space, he complements it.

As I sit on the couch, mug in hand, Gavin says, "The job is yours."

"What?"

"Lead bartender. It's yours."

"What do you mean it's mine?"

He sighs. "Steve is letting go of some servers."

"About fucking time," I mumble, not letting him finish.

"And...I'm taking one of the spots."

I narrow my eyes at him. "Why now? Why like this?"

He shrugs as he takes a sip of coffee. "I don't want to fight anymore. It should have been yours to begin with."

"Well, you're not wrong," I say, but it feels like I'm missing some information. "Did Steve ask you to take the server spot?"

He's suddenly very thirsty for hot coffee, and my mind is quickly putting together the pieces.

"So, I'm second in line for it? What is this—like when you passed up the manager position and they gave it to Steve and he's spent his years repaying you for it?" I shouldn't be upset. I should just take it.

But what about all the hell I got dragged through? The inconvenience I had to be subject to just because. It's all fun and games to everyone else, but I'm supposed to shut up and be grateful.

My coffee is taking on a bitter taste.

"Take the job, T. Fucking take it. It's always been yours," he says adamantly, then for good measure, he adds, "Take the job if it means I can have you."

I raise my eyebrows in disbelief. "A conditional offer, how original."

He stills as he reaches for a sip from his mug.

"And if you can't have me?" I throw out, acid in my tone. Funny how right now he is upsetting my space. Nothing good can last.

"Job is still yours, T," he says quietly, not backing down. "Always will be."

I wanted to fight for it, I want to tell him. I always want to fight. "So, you had to give me the job, instead of letting me rightfully win it?"

"I removed myself from consideration because I had no right to win it," he clarifies, as his eyes hold contact with mine.

I look between them, reaching for understanding. Am I mad at him or mad at Steve? Or am I mad at myself for putting up with Steve's bullshit?

I sigh. "You were..." I swallow. "A formidable opponent."

"Did you just give me another compliment?" he asks, surprised.

I scowl. "Barely."

"Wow."

"A barely formidable opponent."

He reaches for my hand and kisses my palm, moving closer to me on the couch. "So, does this mean I can have you?"

My heart races with panic or hope. I assume it might be the former.

"Thought the rule was until I got lead bartender," I whisper.

"Maybe we can break it," he responds, his voice quiet, looking at me with hope in his eyes.

"Maybe." And I move my body over to snuggle next to his for a while.

"Have you talked to Julie, by the way?" he asks, out of nowhere.

"No, was I supposed to?"

"I heard she's not going to San Diego."

"*What?*"

***

When I get to Julie's place, I don't even bother knocking. I just walk right in and start yelling, my favorite brand of chaos.

Julie, amongst all the family drama from dinner, has decided not to go to San Diego, and that will not fucking stand.

"What the hell are you doing?" I demand.

"What everybody always expects me to do," she answers, defeated. "My whole life has been consumed by guilt. It's always been about the next person I need to appease."

I know the dinner broke her, but I guess I expected more of a fight. "What do you want to do?"

"I don't even know!" she shouts.

Voices start getting louder, making way to finger-pointing.

"You know what the fuck you want, and you need to go out there and do it," I yell.

Our argument reaches screaming levels before Julie cries, more disastrous feelings spill out, and then we fall onto the couch, spent.

"I was so excited when I found out about all this shit you were doing," I say. "You were fucking doing it just like she would have wanted."

"You think so?" Julie's eyes are red, her nose is full of snot.

"*Yes,*" I emphasize. "You're a shit liar and an unconfident lawyer."

She laughs. "You're an asshole."

Before I leave, I walk to the fridge for a drink, reaching for the first LaCroix I see.

"How does Dario drink this shit?" My mouth scrunches in disgust. "Grapefruit? Where? It tastes like a grapefruit farted near some sparkling water and then they canned it. That's what it tastes like."

"I'll let him know how you feel," she says from the couch.

"I'll tell him myself. I don't care."

She laughs softly. "I know you don't."

I sigh, reaching over to give her a hug. All this talk about want, all this fighting, and for what?

"I'll see you soon, okay?"

"Love you, T," she says, and I squeeze her hand before I go.

***

I HOLD THE PAPER bag close to me, and when I walk into the bar, Gavin is already there, restocking for the dinner shift. I'm finally back to work after taking some days to rest my foot. I didn't do a full week like suggested, but enough to get me back on my feet. I quietly set the bag on the counter in front of him then turn to see what else needs to be done.

He stops for a moment, just staring at the bag.

I run through the evening checklist, but he walks over with a grin, and for the first time, I wish I could kiss him right here, out in the open. I wish I could brush the hair off his face, trace his jaw, run my fingertips across his stubble. Everything out in the open.

"Am I interrupting?" Delfi's voice breaks my stare. A reminder that I may not be kissing him out in the open, but I'm certainly acting like it.

I turn to greet her, and her smile tells me she's seen too much.

She's come in for happy hour and grabs a seat before ordering a couple of snacks, but as she does, Julie walks in, surprising us.

"What are you doing here?" I ask. It's not her usual weekend evening.

She introduces us to Larissa, her paralegal, as they sit on the stools. Manny comes by to say hi, and then with all of us as an audience, she blurts out, "We just quit."

My hand freezes mid-air. Delfi balks at them.

"So, we would love some drinks," Julie says. "Larissa, what would you like?"

Larissa responds with something about a glass of wine, but I'm still on the quitting part.

"I'm sorry. Did you say you quit?"

"Like, *your job*?" Delfi is as stunned as me.

"Yes, our terrible job!" Larissa says loudly, which snaps us out of it, and we jump up in celebration.

We throw out congratulations and high fives and talk about what's next.

"Does it involve dancing?" Manny asks boldly.

"Seriously? Does everybody in here know?" Julie asks in disbelief.

But I shrug in response as Manny mutters, "There's no guilt like Hispanic mom guilt."

Except what's next is determined when Julie clears her throat and admits, "I didn't cancel the plane tickets."

My heart stutters over the words, a swell of emotion at the thought of her pushing forward. She wants to do this competition after all, and we're going to get her there. I whip out my phone and do a quick flight search.

Delfi already knows what I'm doing. "I'm so in," she says, giddy with excitement.

"I'll see if Alexis can take your Friday night," Manny offers, reading my mind and checking if she can take the parties Steve put me on.

"I'll take your bar shift," Gavin adds, easily giving me the space to do this.

And when Julie starts to protest, I quickly stop her. "*No.* We are going. We're going to support you because that's how this works and that's what you need."

With this crew of my very best friends, we make plans to get Julie to San Diego. To finally go after what she wants.

She leaves in a rush to go talk with Logan, and Delfi and Larissa stay behind.

"Oh crap. I need somebody to dog sit," Delfi realizes.

"I can dog sit," Larissa chimes in. "I love dogs." She smiles at everybody but lingers on Trevor, who's in the middle of making a cocktail, and he gives a shy smile back.

It's fucking adorable, but good lord, what is in the water?

Delfi and Larissa chat for the next hour or so before Larissa heads out. The bar gets a little busier with our weeknight happy hour crowd, but everything is manageable.

"Gavin?"

A voice I don't recognize cuts through the noise, and I quickly look up.

A woman is at the bar, clearly surprised to see Gavin here.

"Brooke? Hey." He reaches over to give her a hug. "What a surprise. How have you been?"

"Great." She smiles. "How about you?"

"I'm doing really well," he nods with a smile.

Trevor sets down a glass of wine she must have ordered with him, and when she takes it, I notice a large ring on her finger, the lights reflecting off the stone.

I don't miss the way Delfi sits up straighter, eyes moving between Gavin and this new guest.

"Who's that?" I whisper to Trevor.

"Um. That," he says with hesitation, "is his ex-fiancée."

Somewhere in the distance, I think Delfi chokes on a sip of her drink.

"How the hell do you know that?" I ask.

"We talk," Trevor responds, affronted. "He told me one night at the bar."

"And where the hell was I?" I'm talking out loud.

"I don't know, probably in a corner putting a curse on him."

A man in a sharp-dressed suit comes over and gently places a hand on the guest's arm. "Hey, honey. The table is ready."

This feeling is definitely foreign. Not the anger, that one is easy to spot. This is a sort of grief that I didn't get to be first or that I didn't get to have him like that. I don't even want him like that, obviously, but it turns out somebody else got his heart.

This feels embarrassing. This feels unbearably uncomfortable, like I want to crawl out of my skin. As I pulled back the curtain of my privacy, letting him in, he somehow kept the biggest piece from me—his previous engagement. The rug was pulled out from below me, a stupid mistake, leaving me on unsteady ground.

What the fuck am I even doing? Breaking all the rules for this asshole. I never let things get serious, and I'm not going to slip up now.

He catches me staring as she walks away to her table. She's an ex-fiancée with a penchant for well-dressed men. I wonder who broke it off, and why. I'm curious what he's looking for now when he was once in a serious relationship that resulted in him proposing. Who knows what the fuck my face is saying, but it must look distressed enough, because he comes over to me.

"Hey, it's not what you think," he says.

I furrow my brows. "What do I think?"

"Can we talk about this later?" he pleads.

"There isn't anything to talk about, Gavin." I shrug.

"Let me explain."

"You don't have to explain yourself. God." I laugh, but the sound is humorless and dipped in anger. "Trevor, let me take service bar," I say.

"Sure." He nods.

I don't want to talk to anybody right now. I don't want to put on my friendly face and sell. I don't want to throw on my act and smile.

Luckily, Gavin leaves me alone, adhering to Trevor's suggestion.

I need to get the hell out of here. I think I need out of this restaurant. It's finally time.

Alexis and Manny work the large parties, and I handle drinks quickly, with ease. Sam keeps her mistakes to a minimum. For once, Danielle didn't call out, and Kelli and Jordan are up-selling, too. When the rush dies down, Steve calls me to his office.

"Hey, T, I just wanted to tell you I'll be passing lead bartender onto you."

I'm uncomfortably indifferent, reaching for some kind of emotion. "Okay," I say. "Sounds good."

"That's it?" he says with a chuckle. But underneath it I sense the anger, the way he's waiting for me to ceremoniously thank him for picking me.

But I'm still upset, still questioning what I'm even doing

here. Months ago, I would have been fucking thrilled. I would have felt validated and energized. Because, surely, clearly, this was what I wanted. It was what I deserved.

Instead, right now, I feel confused and less than excited. And at the forefront of it, I'm angry that he's taken this away from me too.

***

I ask Derek for a strong drink, and I give him my biggest smile.

"Miss you, T," he says as he sets it down and slides it over to me.

Maybe I'll text him later.

Once I head outside, I notice Dee is out tonight, a rarity, so I move to sit next to her.

"It's nice to see you out, Dee."

"Every now and then," she says, her signature raspy voice. "Gotta keep you all on your toes."

I sigh. "I think I've fucking had it, Dee."

"Yeah?" She takes a drag of her cigarette, thinking it over. "This is it?"

"Think so."

She considers this, blowing out smoke. "The restaurant industry makes you hard. It forces you to be tough and angry. It makes you stand up for yourself in ways that you wouldn't want to otherwise. You form a hard exterior, but it's not who you really are. Don't let them take your softness, T. Hold on to it."

"I don't think I have much of my softness left."

She shakes her head, putting the cigarette out. "You have so much softness in you. And you're deserving of all of it." She squeezes my hand. "Promise me you won't forget that."

"Dee!" Alexis says enthusiastically as she comes over to us.

"With that, I'm out."

"I just got here!" she whines. "One more drink."

"See you soon." She gives us a wink as she gets up, and the crowd waves and shouts their goodbyes.

"Hey," I say to Alexis.

"Hey. Rough night?"

"Something like that." I take a sip of my drink.

The crowd grows bigger, our usual group joining the table, including Gavin and Trevor, who sit down at the opposite end.

Gavin looks over at me, and his eyes are pleading, but for what, I don't know.

I set the rules, I'm not going to be upset about it now.

"So," Alexis starts, and judging by how the night went, I'm not sure if it's going to be great news. "I'm going back to school."

I'm both happy for her and crushed. "For what?"

"Dental hygienist," she says with a smile.

"That's amazing." I try to match it, but it's shaky at best.

"You'll be able to share all your stories, and they won't have a choice but to listen," Manny chimes in, and we laugh.

"It's true, we won't all be here forever," I say, repeating the words Manny once told me.

They nod but don't say anything.

"Thought I had more time."

"More time for what?" Alexis asks.

"To grow up," I say, giving her a sad smile.

For somebody who can't sit still, I really have been stuck in this place. Cecilia's voice is an unwelcome reminder in my head.

This probably isn't what I meant when I wrote that essay junior year about traveling the world and living life unapologetically. Well, maybe it is, but an outsider looking in would probably question why I've been in this shithole for seven years. Why I would let myself get stuck in such a place.

Is this job all I have?

"We've got the rest of our lives to hang out, T. This place will always be ours, but we can have just as much fun outside of it," Manny says.

"Growing up is for suckers," Alexis adds.

"I'm so happy for you," I say, holding her hand. "Don't listen to me. Just had a rough night is all."

"Yeah?"

"Did you know Gavin has an ex-fiancée?" I throw out.

Their wide stares are answers enough, and they can't help themselves when they both look over at him on the opposite side of our table.

"Yeah. I didn't either. She came in today. Accidental meeting." I wave it away. "So, anyway."

"Wanna talk about it?" Manny suggests.

"God, no."

Alexis looks between us before she says, "And why does this matter?"

"He didn't feel the need to share any of that information with me."

"But did you even care to ask? Did you even *care*? Or were you keeping him at arm's length in your bed?"

I give her a look.

"No shame." She puts her hands up. "Never shame or judgment from me, babe."

"She might have a point," Manny winces. "We love you, but not only do you keep people from knowing about you, but you make it so that you don't have to know about them either."

"I think I need another drink."

When I get up to go to Derek at the bar, an influx of foreign emotions practically attacks me.

What does it say about me if I feel left behind by Alexis's news?

What does it say about me that I feel uncomfortable about Gavin and an ex-fiancée?

Of course, Manny and Alexis are right. I never let anybody in.

That wasn't the plan. Nothing was serious. And on top of it all, I feel betrayed. The liquor uncomfortably lingers in the pit of my stomach.

"Another one, T?" Derek asks.

"I don't think so." I change my mind. "Just cash me out."

"It's on the house," he says then leans against the bar top toward me. "Want to come over after this?"

Nothing has ever been less appealing. I just want to get the hell out of this noisy bar, crawl out of these uncomfortable clothes, and go the fuck to sleep. Alone.

"No, Derek." I shake my head, and maybe he sees something in my face, because he just nods. And I don't think he plans on asking me ever again.

Thirty-One
AGOSTINA

"Can we talk?" Gavin approaches me in the parking lot as everybody is leaving the Knotty Bar. Undoubtedly the worst place to argue.

"There's nothing to say, Gavin."

"I'm not a mind reader, and I have no intention of being one, so we're going to talk about how we feel."

His voice is calm, talking me off a ledge, but all it does it piss me off more.

"You sure spent a lot of time getting to know me, and you couldn't even tell me about yourself," I say.

He throws his hands up. "You never wanted to know."

"You never had a problem sharing things whether I asked about them or not," I throw back.

He sighs like he knows I'm right. "I'm sorry I didn't tell you about Brooke. It didn't seem like something you wanted to know about, considering you were so set on defining the rules of whatever the fuck is between us."

"Don't turn this around on me." I know I sound ridiculous, but none of my feelings make any sense as it is.

"Brooke and I were together for a couple of years. The proposal wasn't what I wanted, it was what she wanted. And then we realized we couldn't do it, so we broke it off."

I lean against my car, keys in my hand keeping my fingers busy.

"What else do you want to know?"

There are so many things I want to ask. So many questions I could never get myself to speak out loud.

Did you love her? Not that I care.

Do you want to get married again? I don't.

Why am I so mad about this? I have no idea.

"She married a doctor. She's happy, and so am I." He looks at me intensely, fire in his eyes, screaming for something. "Ask me if I care. Ask me if I care about any of it but you. Ask me if anything matters to me like you do."

My mouth is painfully dry.

"Tell me how you feel, T."

"You know how I feel," I manage to say.

"No, I don't. I need you to tell me. I need to *hear it.* Please."

I like spending time with him and talking to him. I find myself wanting to invite him over. I search for ways to be with him. I feel safe and at peace. But all that means is a relationship, and I know where they lead. And I see me losing myself already—constantly thinking about him, letting my walls down and allowing myself to be surprised by a fucking ex-fiancée.

I think of my mother, who settled and sat silently, watching everything pass her by. Who's own relationship became a guideline of what not to do. I don't want to be my mother. Every step of my life ensures that, but what if I'm slowly becoming her anyway? What if I'm forgetting who I am?

This feels like I'm drowning, fighting a hurricane of bad

decisions, and I need it to stop.

"I'm taking this trip and who knows what's going to happen when I get back," I tell him.

He rears his head back in surprise. "What—What does that mean?"

"It means…" It means I need to cut this now before it gets any messier than it's already been. It means I need to stop this before we both tumble down a rabbit hole and there's no turning back. "It means I was never going to stay, Gavin," I whisper. "And you knew that."

"Are you talking about The Ivy? Or about us?"

"You can take the job."

"Jesus Christ, it was never about the job. It was always about being near you."

"What the hell are you doing with me? Why don't you go find somebody else to marry? It's clearly what you want. Go find somebody that you can confine to a house under your thumb and suck the life out of her."

"I'm not your parents, T," he says harshly as he shakes his head.

"Keep my parents out of your fucking mouth," I shoot back.

This thing with Gavin got out of hand, but I need to let it go now. I need to let him go so he can go be with somebody else, somebody better fit for what he wants.

"Come on, Gavin. You know I'm not what you need."

"Don't do that. Don't fucking do that, T."

"I'm not doing anything."

"Stop fighting with me," he pleads. "Stop picking at everything because you're scared."

"This wasn't what we agreed to," I say, voice firm. "This wasn't supposed to happen like this."

"Yeah well, maybe you're right. Maybe I didn't agree to this—this silence. This secrecy. Maybe I want to shout out how much I want you. I want to scream how much you make me feel. Maybe I want to let this whole fucking world know how much I fucking love you."

I've never heard him this loud, this angry. A contradicting thing when he's telling me he loves me.

"Do what you want, but I'm not letting this go. I'm not giving up on any of it." He's adamant.

"Well, I want you to," I argue.

"Well, too fucking bad!" he shouts back. "You're not going to push me away. Push everybody else away if you want to, but not me. I'm here."

"You're always here!" I throw my hands up. "You're relentless, and I'm suffocating," I yell. "You want more than I'm willing to give."

His eyebrows lift. "Do you really feel that way?"

No. "Yes."

I can feel it when he severs ties, like a deep ache in my bones, a wildfire of pain running its course through me.

"Fine. Go ahead and run. You're so good at it," he throws back at me.

I can't act affected now. I can't show the tears forming, or my hands shaking. "Yeah, I will, thanks," I answer, opening my car door to go.

I'm always quick on the trigger, quick to shoot back, not realizing how defeated he looks. Realizing too late how his eyes have turned sad and pleading. And how the ribs that have some-how held me are cracking.

Joy is an uncomfortable emotion. It's easier to sit in the sadness or the unstable because it's more familiar. Allowing the joy is much harder.

Everything is better when it's temporary, when I don't get attached, when I don't have to fight about my life with some-body else.

But if this is what I want, why the fuck does it hurt so much?

Thirty-Two
GAVIN

BROOKE AND I WERE together during a time in my life that I vaguely recognize.

I wasn't really myself back then, and our relationship was built on just going through the motions. And when we talked about the next step, it seemed like the right thing to do. So, we looked at rings, and I blindly proposed, and everything seemed as it should be.

Except it felt confusing, and I couldn't shake the feeling that it just wasn't what I wanted.

But I couldn't define what I *did* want and so I had a hard time letting it go.

One rare night I found myself out with Logan, attending one of his dance competitions. He'd built a rallying community around him, one that thrived on love and respect for each other. His partner Tara was a force, and I was so deeply proud of him in that moment. So unbelievably in awe of him, and I realized then that while I wasn't entirely sure of what I did want, maybe it was a little close to what he had: friendships and a beloved community. And somebody to share it with who was real, who I could talk to.

Brooke and I talked shortly after and realized we were both

barely in it, so we mutually broke it off and went our separate ways. I worried I would grieve some part of a life I'd never have, but all I felt was relief.

She moved out, and then I followed, leaving behind our shared apartment and moving in with Logan instead.

I heard she got married from some old mutual acquaintances, and I felt nothing but happiness for her, that she got what she wanted.

And as for me, I found what I wanted, too.

But I'd be lying if I said I didn't feel the grief of it sneaking up on me some days, wondering how to make any of it work.

I never thought to mention Brooke because it was in the past, something we never talked about, something we agreed didn't matter.

Agostina is the only one that's ever mattered, and everything feels like it's crumbling around me. This is the elusive grief I'd been expecting to feel.

Delfina comes over to our side of the table, drink in hand.

"Did T leave?" she asks, looking around.

"Yeah, you just missed her," I answer.

"Want to play, Delfi?" Trevor asks, motioning to the open pool table.

She shakes her head. "No. I think Manny wanted to, though."

As Manny comes by and picks up a cue, she sits close to me.

"Hey," she says quietly.

"What a mess, huh?" I lightly tease, but it doesn't land. "You ever wonder if she loves you?" I ask, but the question doesn't come out quite right.

She lifts her head in surprise. "Of course, she loves us."

"How do you know that?" I might be begging for answers.

Delfina sighs as she shakes her head. "She's a tough cookie, but that doesn't mean she doesn't know how to love people. She knows how to love them so deeply. She has such a big heart, an expanding heart, for the people in her life. But those are heavy words, you know? I'll be honest, I don't think her parents ever said those words growing up. So sometimes I love you sounds a lot like *come with me on this trip. I bought you a croissant from that bakery you like because I passed by and thought of you. Watch out for that corner.*"

"'Here's a Band-Aid,'" I add, not realizing it. Speaking out loud.

"Here's a Band-Aid," she repeats with a small smile and a nod.

"'Stay the night.'"

Her eyes soften, and her hand goes to her heart, as she nods some more. "Yes."

"Her mother, my aunt, God bless her, I think became so codependent on her husband. So, what did Agos do? She went all the way to the other end of it. She became so independent that I think she forgot that she's allowed to want somebody to share her life with. Like, that's okay. There doesn't need to be marriage involved. Who cares? It's your life. And you are allowed to build your life how you want. I mean, hell, she preaches about it to everybody else. You'd think she'd take her own advice."

"She doesn't think she's allowed that," I say.

Delfi takes a sip of her drink, shaking her head as she does.

"No, she doesn't."

"My own fault." I sigh. "I wanted to give her everything, but it was at the expense of her independence. Her strong will."

"It's gonna be all right," she says with her ever-present positivity, the gift she offers everybody. But then her mouth turns down at the corners. "Just...just don't give up on her, okay?"

I feel the longing in my heart, the never-ending want, the love for her. "I don't think I ever could."

Thirty-Three
AGOSTINA

SAN DIEGO IS A beautiful city, but not beautiful enough that it can fix my stupid broken heart. All of this feels stupid and unnecessary. Who the hell told me to get involved with a coworker like this?

Delfi doesn't pry much during the trip, letting me be as we explore the beaches and the taco stands. The weather is in the sixties this time of year, comfortably cool enough to enjoy.

When we finally get to watch the competition, I can tune out every bad thing and focus on the reason we're here—Julie in a remarkable dress and Celestina's magical shoes.

As I watch Julie dance, I'm brought back to watching my grandmother, the unbridled joy that ran through her feet. I witness that same joy in Julie now. The unwavering talent, the bravery she exhibited in coming here.

They used to tell me I was so brave, so open to adventure at every turn. But the truth is, I just got really good at running.

Just like Gavin said.

Back in the hotel room, the three of us sprawl out on the bed. Delfi and I ordered room service earlier, opting to celebrate and enjoy our time quietly, and Julie came in to join us.

I pull out the travel journal to add to notes about San Diego, not in order, but it doesn't matter much anymore, does it? I don't have many places left.

And there's one I've been dying to get to.

"I think it's time for me to just skip ahead," I tell them.

They move next to me as I open the book to the last page, her favorite place.

Julie lets out a soft gasp.

"*Ohh*," Delfina says softly, a knowing smile on her face.

And I set the journal down as I mutter, "Son of a bitch."

There, on the very last page, set in the middle, is a picture of her house, humble but lively. Plants decorating the front porch, two rocking chairs placed side by side. And standing in front of it, my grandmother, smiling wide, and my grandfather, arm wrapped around her. Like *look at how lucky I am. Look at this life I've gotten to live along this beautiful woman. Look at how perfect this is.*

And underneath the picture, in her loopy cursive:

My home will always be my favorite place in this world. My home is and always will be next to him.

A reminder that the joy of traveling this world is certainly something, but maybe having somebody to share it with makes it shine that much more.

"He biked twenty miles just to see her." Delfina shrugs. "Are we surprised?"

"Ugh," I groan. "Well, this is it, then." The end of the journal.

"How apropos," Julie says, smile on her face. "What are you going to do now?"

The burning question. "Well, I'll finish it. I still need to go to Portland. But, after that, I'll make my own plans, I guess."

"Make them with him," Delfi says, nudging my elbow.

The end of one journal—one journey—and the beginning of another. God, that's so symbolic. I almost hate it.

"I don't want to lose myself," I tell them quietly, admitting my fears. "I don't want to change."

"But you're not changing, T," Delfi says with a shake of her head. "Not who you are inside or otherwise. You're just...*amplifying*. You're getting louder and brighter and flourishing. It's not change, it's growth. And it's been a revelation to watch."

"You've always been the best one out of us, you know that, don't you?" Julie sets her hand on my shoulder. "And maybe you bring out the best in him, too."

I am allowed to grow, I'm allowed to evolve. I always thought it was aimed toward work, but in reality, it was for my life.

I flip the page over in habit before closing the journal up, but I catch some writing on the back of the last page.

Agostina, I hope you travel the world. And I hope you are brave enough to accept whatever it is you want.

Goddammit, I really don't want to cry right now.

"Oh my God," Delfi whispers as she reads it, tears starting to pool in her eyes.

Mine well up with traitorous tears anyway, and I quickly wipe them away. I need to get out of here for a moment, so I set the journal down and walk out to the hotel balcony.

Six floors up is enough distance from the rest of the world for now, but shortly after, Julie steps outside to join me.

"How did you stay?" I ask her.

She gives me a kind smile then shakes her head. "I stayed

because I was scared. I stayed because I thought I had to. You have always been strong enough to go after what you want. You built an incredible life for yourself, and you're going to keep doing it. I promise."

I spent so much of my life giving into whatever pleasure I wanted, a selfish journey. Every pleasure except love. I was never quite brave enough for that.

And it hit me like a ton of bricks in the form of one very charismatic, very loving, very perfect bartender.

One night, many years ago, Delfi asked us what we thought falling in love felt like. Inconvenient, I'd said.

Joke's on me, isn't it? 'Cause he's been the most inconvenient thing of all.

***

Julie and Logan decide to stay a little longer in San Diego, but Delfi and I need to head back home. Our flight has a layover in Houston, but we make do.

Once we find our gate, Delfi walks over to grab us coffee and snacks, one of her favorite things to do in the airport. When she eventually makes it back, she quickly passes me the coffee cup, but she looks like hell. It was an early flight, I know, but still.

"You okay?" I extend my hand out to grab it.

She breathes out. "I just saw John."

"John?"

"He was with his girlfriend. Oh God, there he goes."

John gives us a wave, one that holds years of yearning, as he stands next to, I assume, his girlfriend.

"Oh shit, it *is* John," I mumble under my breath, eyes wide as he walks up to us.

"How's it going, Agostina?" he says.

"Well, this is a surprise," I say. We've known this kid since we were eight years old, but I can't remember the last time I saw him.

The flight attendant gets on the loudspeaker. "Flight now boarding for Florida."

"That's us," I announce, and we gather our bags. "Always good to see you, John, even if it is random as hell."

"Likewise," he says with a laugh. But he's not looking at me when he says it. Then he slowly, almost apprehensively, moves in to give Delfi a hug and mumbles, "See you around, Fifi."

We watch him walk away with his slightly confused girlfriend in tow.

"Goddammit," I mutter as I close my eyes. "The universe is really beating me over the head with it today. Delfi, I know the rest of the flight isn't going to be easy, so hold my hand if you need to or order a movie if you need to, but I just want you to know that I'm finally ready to go home."

She turns to look at me, eyes sad but clinging to hope, and she takes hold of my hand, squeezing as we board the plane.

Thirty-Four
GAVIN

I'VE SEEN A LOT of my brother's competitions and I can count on one hand the ones I've had to miss, but this one I'd consider a gift. Agostina needed to be there more than I did. She needed to support Julie, she needed time away with her cousins, and as much as it pains me to say, she needed time away from me.

"You upset you're missing out on San Diego?" Trevor asks.

Another shift down, one without her.

"Nah, I'm all right." I take a sip of my beer. "She needed it more than I did."

"Well, sounds like you both got hurt."

I nod, sighing. "Something like that."

He shakes his head and puts his hand on my shoulder. "I'm here for you. But also, I told you so."

"T was right. You *are* a pain in the ass."

He laughs quietly.

Alexis brings over a large platter of wings, setting it in the center of the table. Manny comes behind her, snagging one from the middle. Trevor grabs one, and I join in, picking one up for myself.

"God, what a night, huh?" Alexis says, taking a sip of her drink and lamenting about her night.

It was unexpectedly busy, the kind that surprises you and throws you into a tailspin. T would have handled it perfectly, I think, smiling to myself.

Manny and Trevor laugh about their night, sharing stories of their shift, and I keep quiet, watching them. Months ago, this place was a foreign concept. This group was suspicious of me, wondering why Steve offered me the position he did. But now, I'm as much a part of this as anyone else. It's familiar, it's comfortable, it's the very thing I've longed for.

There's still one piece of it missing—the heart of it, the part that makes everything feel alive. I ache for her to come back.

"You doing okay, Gavin?" Alexis asks.

They've all been worried about me, checking in on me more than usual. But I'm okay. More than okay, I realize.

"You know, when I first started working at The Ivy, I didn't know how it was going to go. I didn't know what it would mean for me. But you all welcomed me in—well, most of you," I say, and they laugh. I rub the condensation off my glass, keeping busy while I speak my peace. "Some days I think about how happy I am that I got laid off. I'm happy I got to meet you. And I'm happy you're in my life. You're like the family I never had."

"We love you, Gavin," Alexis says softly.

"We do," Manny agrees. "And she does, too," he adds, and we all know who he means.

I sigh, then down the last sip of of my beer.

"Don't they come back tonight?" Trevor asks.

"Think so," Alexis says. "Another round, anybody?"

"Not for me." I shake my head. "It's time for me to head home."

I leave the Knotty Bar early, not interested in closing it down tonight. I take a quick shower once I get to my place, letting myself get settled into the quiet—TV on, mug of tea in hand.

I've been trying my hand at drinking tea before bed, calming me and lulling me to sleep. But as I settle in, there's what sounds like a bunch of uncoordinated taps at my front door.

Thirty-Five
AGOSTINA

I TRY MY OWN hand at a rhythmic knock, but it kind of sounds rocks hitting a door. I lift my hand to try again when the door opens and Gavin emerges.

I keep my palm out, stretched toward his face, not even letting him get a word in before I do.

"You've pissed me off relentlessly. You've annoyed the shit out of me."

He rears his head back. "Did you come to insult me?"

"But you've also made me feel less alone. You've made me feel understood," I keep going. "You've made me feel so many big things that I didn't think I could possibly handle. Even now, I think I'm going to throw it all up. But I'm here. And my heart is practically on a platter for you as I stand here. And I need you to put me out of my misery a little bit, because God, this is awful."

"I—"

"I'm not done." I shake my head as I continue. "I don't give a shit about Brooke. Sorry. Or the lead bartender job, because I'm going to leave. Or what we watch on TV, I've decided. Because all that matters is that you're with me. I don't tolerate anybody, but I tolerate you."

A smile slowly unfurls on his face. "This is really romantic, T-pain."

"I'm a pain in the ass, I know that, but you make me feel like I'm not. And that's something."

"That's something," he repeats with a grin.

"But—But anyway, the point is, I don't like you. I don't. And you know that. But what you need to hear is that I don't like you because I love you. So there. I love you. What a mess."

This smile is frame-worthy, memory-worthy. It's close to the picture I have of us on the Ferris wheel, the one I pinned to my wall in a confusing, surprising move. This smile is, and always has been, just for me. How desperately I wanted to believe it at the beginning, and how sure I feel seeing it now.

"I love you, too," he says.

Hearing him say that may be the best thing I've ever heard. God, I never thought those words could sound like that. So...defining. And life-changing. So sure. And I guess I can reason that if I feel that way when he says it, then he must feel that way when I say it to him.

"But I don't want to get married," I blurt out.

"Okay, I don't either." He shrugs with that same smile. "I don't need marriage or a wedding. I just need you for the rest of my life."

"I don't need anything," I say softly. "But I want you. I choose you, Gavin."

He takes two steps toward me, leaning down to press his lips to mine. His answering kiss is everything I love about his mouth. Soft and sweet and passionate. He holds me close, and I feel his heartbeat working overtime. Mine must be a close second.

"What took you so long, T?" He breathes in the scent of my hair, as his hand cradles the nape of my neck.

"I had a layover in Houston."

He laughs softly, and I still love the sound of it, the feel of it against my bones.

"Bye, lovebirds!" Delfi screams from the driver's seat.

"Is that Delfina?" he asks, surprised.

"We just landed and drove here from the airport. Also, Logan is still in San Diego, so I'm spending the night." I hold up my luggage that I had set to the side.

His smile grows bigger. "Is that right?"

"I want to see your place, too."

He opens the door wider for me to come in, and I take it all in. Nowhere near as colorful as my place, but cozy and comfortable and clean. Shoes by the door, a mug on the coffee table, Netflix on TV.

"And what's this about you leaving The Ivy?"

That place was a big part of my life, but it wasn't so much the place as the people around me. The ones at the heart of the restaurant. Maybe I'll miss walking around the bar and walking to the storage closet in the back. I'll miss walking past the line cooks and saying hi to Hector every day. I'll definitely miss working with Manny and Trevor and Alexis.

But it feels good to move on. Like I can finally allow myself to.

"It's time," I tell him.

"I'm happy for you. Whatever you choose to do, I'm here."

"And it's not suffocating," I clarify, aiming to correct my accusations. "You're not...relentless. Well, you are. But I like it."

He grins. "I know."

His arm wraps around my waist, pulling me closer. He kisses me again, and this kiss is sweet. Grounding. Scary, but I'm learning to be brave when it comes to him. This kiss is hopes and wishes and dreams.

When he pulls back, he smiles, and it makes me dizzy—the blinding light of it. It feels like something sliding into place. There's a small part of my brain, one I'm trying to shut up, telling me I need to run. I need to get out of this before I fall too deep and I'll never make it out.

"I don't know what happens after this, Gavin," I admit. "I've never had to try after this, and I've never wanted to. But you make me want so much, and I guess I'm willing to try. Right now. For you."

"I love you, Agostina," he says, and I may never get used to how wonderful my name sounds on his lips. "That's all that matters. The rest we'll figure out together."

The bigger part is ready for me to accept what I truly want. To try on bravery for size. And to build my own adventure with him.

I can't wait.

EPILOGUE

Agostina, two years later

"Come *on*, my cousin is going to kill us if we miss this flight."

"I hardly think she would kill us."

"Oh sorry, did I say she would? I meant me. Now move."

"But let's just have a little fun before we go." He pulls at my waist, bringing me closer to kiss my neck.

My palms meet his chest. "And please make sure you have your passport."

"I've got it," he says in between kisses.

"Great. Car's here."

"Fine," he playfully rolls his eyes. "Let's go to a wedding."

The airport is bustling, but we manage to find most of our group. Alexis grabbed some snacks, Manny is probably three margaritas in, trying to quell his nerves before the nine hour red-eye, and Trevor is walking over with Larissa now.

Travel for Gavin is still exciting, still something novel. Especially since it's attached to fun, not work. And he's never flown out of the country before, so this will be its own experience.

The past couple of years have been a lesson in bravery, in taking what I want.

During one of my busy shifts at The Ivy, Carol had passed me a business card for the food and beverage director of Regency on the Water, the luxury hotel on the beach.

"Call her," she'd adamantly said, and I tucked it into my pocket and let it be.

But when I was doing my laundry, emptying pockets as I went, I stumbled upon it and I wondered, what did I have to lose?

Turns out they were looking for a bar manager for a new concept restaurant. I said no at first, not wanting to get thrown into an uncertain business, something new and unestablished. But she was persistent, and honest. She was willing to be flexible, and she was willing to offer a lot.

She'd heard a lot about me, she said, from Carol, among others, and she believed in me.

So, I went for another interview and became bar manager of their new beachfront restaurant. With a great team under me, flexibility to live my life, and health benefits I can't complain about.

They also offered me a 401k, so I have one of those now, too. How annoying.

"You want anything?" Gavin asks me. "I'm going to grab a tea."

"A decaf coffee, if they have it."

Gavin and I went to Portland together, the final trip from the journal, and sharing it with him was more emotional than I expected it to be. Symbolic of something, I'm sure. We both had never been, but we both fell in love with the city. My grandmother said she didn't play favorites too often, but she really loved Portland.

"Has anybody heard from Julie?" Manny asks.

"She flew in yesterday," I answer. "She said everything looks beautiful."

My family and I still do Sunday dinners, but now we have extra guests join us. Logan loved it instantly, felt right at home with everybody. Gavin felt like a fish out of water, but he's managed to slowly settle in, too. Especially with his brother nearby.

I never thought it would matter to me who joined these dinners, but having Gavin next to me has made me feel less alone. Like I don't have to fight by myself, I don't have to go through any of it by myself.

We still meet Alexis, Manny, and Trevor for drinks on occasion. Trevor started a new band, and we watch him play at local dive bars whenever we can. Alexis is thriving in dental, sharing way too many stories about herself, and dating somebody new. And Manny started teaching a year ago.

As for The Ivy, it's still there. Trevor works the bar and Gavin, well, he took the lead bartender position. I gave him my blessing.

Delfi, Julie and I get together for happy hours whenever our schedules allow, and I always make it a point to say hi to Hector and Dee, but some of the line cooks and servers have moved on, the rotating door of the hospitality industry.

And as for Steve, he got fired about year ago. Nobody was surprised.

The airport intercom comes to life, the attendant on the loudspeaker calling out, "Flight now boarding nonstop to Buenos Aires, Argentina."

"Let's go, team," Alexis says, energized and gathering all her belongings. She's got a travel pillow, an extra pillow, a blanket, and an eye mask. God bless her.

"Hey T, we're gone for a week. How many pairs of underwear did you pack?" Trevor asks.

I let out a laugh. "Guess."

"Nine," he answers.

"Twelve," Manny suggests.

Gavin looks on, confused.

"Fifteen," Alexis says, shuffling her luggage over.

"Alexis wins." I give her a high five, and everybody else looks mildly horrified.

"Fifteen?" Gavin asks. "Are you okay?"

My answering sigh is a happy one, a satisfied one. "I have never been better," I answer, and I lift up on my toes to give him one very big, probably inappropriate kiss.

When I pull away, he smiles. *Mine*, I think. I get to kiss him out in the open now, gently touch his stubble, brush his hair out of his eyes.

No, I've never been better as I stand here with him and my very best friends, as we head to my beautiful birth city, to see one of the best people in the world get married.

ACKNOWLEDGEMENTS

First and foremost, for Stefani. If you ask her, she'll tell you how we met – how I disliked her, and she eventually wore me down. I will neither confirm nor deny, but I will say that she's the Alexis to my Agostina, and she helped me immensely with this book. I've been dreaming of these characters for years now, and she's been answering my late night nonsensical texts since then. Well, about the book. She's been answering my nonsensical texts about other things for much longer than that.

Brian, who is always one of the first to read my books, whose support means so much to me, and who has – up until now – shared my books with his mom. Sorry, Brian's mom, you don't need to read this one.

Kristen, the first person to read my drafts and tell me if they're trash or not. She has yet to tell me they're trash, but maybe one day. Your support and your enthusiasm for my writing is one of the very best things, and I'm so grateful for you.

Sara, my teenage pen-pal and one of the best writers I know. Thank you for your words of wisdom, and your encouragement.

Jane, if we're not lamenting about social media, what are we doing! Thanks for always listening to me vent.

The Pen Pals! I have been lucky enough to get added to a small author group chat with some of the most delightful, talented authors I know. Every day I wonder how I managed to squeeze my way in, and every day I'm grateful for it. Thank you to Janine, Abigail, Katy, and Colleen. You are the very best.

Nicole, Katie, Patricia. Friends and family that give me love and support year round.

Lucy, as always, for being an absolute delight to work with and giving me the cover of my dreams!

Allie, my former editor who was privy to my emotional breakdown, and offered more grace than I probably deserve.

Andrea, my new editor who took this project on within a time crunch. Thank you for your flexibility and your work!

A very special shout out to indie bookstores championing for indie authors, indie authors that offer support and community, and libraries – especially my local one, doing the hard work, supporting local authors like me.

To you, dear reader, for picking this book up.

And Brad, my forever favorite line cook, who patiently deals with my never-ending time behind a laptop and brings me coffee with inappropriate notes on them.

ABOUT THE AUTHOR

Natalia writes contemporary romance featuring characters in their thirties and all their emotional baggage. Born in Argentina, now residing in Florida, she spent over a decade in the culinary field, but now spends her days wrangling kids and writing love stories. She loves a good cheeseburger, dogs, and has a freezer full of ice cream.

Find her on social media @nw.writes